None of us pays to much attention to Ring. Of course, we don't think we have to chase him away from the water. We just watch as he walks deeper into the river. First it is up to his knees, little ripples from a passing boat washing up against his legs. But he doesn't turn around to come back.

Ring just keeps wading. The sun is dribbling down, lighting his face, all squinted up and laughing. He suddenly goes deeper, and he keeps wading until he slides down beneath the water, under a big wave. A second before he slips under, he looks back at us.

He doesn't pop back up. He's nowhere in sight.

DANGLING

BY LILLIAN EIGE

ALADDIN PAPERBACKS

New York London Toronto Sydney Singapore

First Aladdin Paperbacks edition September 2003

Copyright © 2001 by Lillian Eige

ALADDIN PAPERBACKS
An imprint of Simon & Schuster
Children's Publishing Division
1230 Avenue of the Americas
New York, NY 10020

Also available in an Atheneum hardcover edition
Designed by Anne Scatto and Sonia Chaghatzbanian
The text of this book was set in Perpetua.

Printed in the United States of America
10 9 8 7 6 5 4 3 2 1

The Library of Congress has cataloged the hardcover edition as follows:
Eige, Lillian.
Dangling / by Lillian Eige.
p. cm.
Summary: Eleven-year-old Ben recalls his relationship with his unusual friend Ring, who walked into the river and disappeared one day.
ISBN 0-689-83581-7 (hc., alk. paper)
[1. Friendship—Fiction. 2. Missing persons—Fiction. 3. Foster home care—Fiction.]
I. Title.
PZ7.E3437 Dan 2001
[Fic]—dc21
00-020006
ISBN 0-689-86350-0 (Aladdin pbk.)

In loving memory of my mother,
Lillian NcNary Hunt, and Gaylerd, my husband.

Chapter 1

It starts this morning when I'm out running. I swear I can hear Ring thumping along beside me, just like he did a couple of days ago. We always ran like that, side by side, touching and bumping each other. And next I think I hear him laughing right in the middle of a bunch of kids walking down the street, kind of hee-hawing like he does when he gets out of control. It's worse tonight in the dark when I feel him close, trotting beside me, wherever I go, his sneakers slapping the pavement, and I can hear him snickering, snorting like a suffocating dog.

But when I turn to find him nobody is there.

If that sounds crazy and anyone thinks I must be cracking up, well that is too darn bad. It's something I have to figure out for myself. All I am trying to do is get everything straight in my head about Ring. So far my head feels like a roller-coaster running wild.

It was only yesterday when everything was just hunky-dory. Same old thing like always. We went on a picnic out to the woods along the Shellrock River. It was going to be a real fun day. Of course we were all there: Ring and me, his folks, Purcell and Josie, and Kate and Mattie.

The sun was shooting beams through the trees like spinning tennis balls, the trees leaning side-ways in the breeze as if they expected to retrieve them. Once in a while one of us had to chase Mattie away from the water. My grandma is old and fearless.

Ring's mom, Josie, packed a lunch, enough for an army. When she took the lid off the picnic basket the smell was enough to knock you off your feet: ham sandwiches, hunks of cheese, beans, peach pie. Kate brought a big blanket, big enough for all of us to sit on. She made us wait until she smoothed it out to the corners.

While we are eating it gets quiet, then when we've eaten so much we can't roll over and the talking and the laughing starts, Ring is the noisiest. We have to listen to his story about his kooky friend Fox, who Ring says went to the park whenever he got hungry just to beg leftovers from people's picnics. "He got so fat he could barely walk."

"Too much ice cream?" I ask. "Too bad for being a pig."

"Hey, you do what you've got to do. Ice cream melts. You can't take it with you." Ring is hoisting up onto his big long legs. "Fox was real picky. One swing through the park and he could tell where the best food was. He had the nose of a beagle. He could smell hamburgers cooking on the other side of the park. That's a real talent."

"Nobody ever stop him, maybe get arrested?" Ring's dad, Purcell, asks, looking suspicious. He is always asking Ring the hard questions.

Ring glances at him for a second, like he is not sure what to say. He shakes his head. "But Fox said you have to know what you're doing. Stay out of trouble. It ain't easy, he says."

While he is talking Ring is trying to balance a piece of peach pie in his hand, but it's leaking down the front of his shirt anyway. The wind is blowing Kate's short hair straight up, and everyone is laughing.

I get caught up in the whole scene like I'm watching a movie. If I ever take a picture to keep forever, this will be the one, with the big old tree limbs over us and the light shining off the river.

Then old Ring starts worrying about his messy shirt, and he rolls up his pants and walks down to the river and splashes water down his front.

None of us pay too much attention, too full to move. Of course, we don't think we have to chase him away from the water like we do Mattie. We just watch as he walks deeper into the river. First it is up to his knees, little ripples from a passing boat washing up against his legs. But he doesn't turn around to come back.

Josie yells at him, "You shouldn't go in the water so soon after you eat!"

But Ring just keeps wading. The sun is dribbling down, lighting his face, all squinted up and laughing. He suddenly goes deeper, and he keeps wading until he slides down beneath the water, under a big wave. A second before he slips under he looks back at us.

We stare at the river waiting for him to come up. He could swim like a fish. It seemed a whole minute we sat there stunned. You know how it is: you don't believe what you are seeing. One minute he is there laughing, and the next, gone. Then it hits us. He doesn't pop back up. He's nowhere in sight.

We all start yelling and running like a bunch of crazies. Grabbing one another's hands, we plunge into the water, Mattie hanging on to Kate and me.

The fire department comes in about thirty minutes, as fast as we can get to a telephone to call them. They drag up and down the river until dark. Everybody is hollering, making so much noise we couldn't have heard Ring if he had been screaming his head off.

I just want them to be quiet and listen, the same as me. I walk along the riverbank and watch. Kate says I shouldn't.

"Let's go home," she says. "You're shaking."

The next morning was when I decided to start running early every day, always first along the riverbank. Goofy, but I think I am going to find Ring. It is so quiet there, even though I know they are still dragging below where we had our picnic. This morning the wind is kind of blowing, and I hear a bird off somewhere.

I can't stop thinking, how could he just disappear like that? No sign of him, and it isn't a real deep river, maybe kind of wide. Kate had hung on to me yesterday so I couldn't go back in, and Purcell couldn't swim.

And when I think about it, it gives me a headache, like something eating a hole in my brains. I just can't figure out why he didn't come up. And I'm running and running and I suddenly feel so sick, my legs just fold up under me. I think I see his face bobbing in the water, racing me, laughing, and I think I'm going batty.

Chapter 2

The very first time I saw Ring I thought my eyes were playing tricks on me, on my brain, too. It seems he dropped out of nowhere down to the middle of our town, Green Hills, into a cemetery pond alongside a pair of swans.

Anyway, that's where I found him on the way home from school. I was taking a short cut through the cemetery, and I saw this kid, mud to his waist, wet pants hanging from his hips, no shirt, and shaking like a wet dog. At first I figured it must be some dumb kind of April Fools' joke, that he got dunked by somebody.

But then I notice he was bending over in the water trying to get a remote-control boat untangled from the lily pads. When I saw the swans ready to attack, I can't help waiting to see what was going to happen. Once one of the nasty swans got a hold of him, too bad.

When he spots me he ducks like he's trying to hide behind one of the lilies. Then he sees the swans. They're heading straight for him, and he yells at me, "Hey, man! Quit your laughing! Get those crazy swans out of here! What are you waiting for?"

I should have clobbered him. Instead, when I see this idiot with big teeth and long hair blowing in his eyes about to have a nervous breakdown, I start yelling and clapping my hands, and once I'm sure the swans are leaving I wade in.

From the beginning Ring could startle me into doing something stupid that I didn't plan on, like wading into that muddy pond with my school shoes on, two feet of water and about six feet of mud.

I figure he's plenty dumb, and a runt, too. I suppose that's just because I'm a runt and because of the way he squats down in the pond. But then he unfolds and stands up straight out of the water. He's so tall I can't believe it, and no bigger around than Mattie's little finger. A complete disaster.

"Hey there!" he yells at me as I'm trying to

crawl up the slippery bank. He hands me the control to the boat and lets me run it a few times.

And that is that. I don't see him for the rest of the summer. I don't even know his name. When school starts I look for him. I try to describe him and it's hard. No one seems to have heard of him until I run into Homer, a kid in my class whose dad is head of the city's waste department, which of course gives him access to information some of the rest of us don't have. His dad claims to have seen him around town early in the mornings, running. He never got a good look because the kid was always going so fast, except he was so ungodly tall and skinny.

Then the stories start coming fast. Every kid has a different story. They make him sound like a man from Mars. Probably all made up, because I am the only one who claims to have come face-to-face with him, except Homer's dad.

Some of the kids are saying that he moved here from New York City, or Cincinnati, Ohio, some place a thousand miles away. My own guess is maybe he really did fall off a planet. Anyway, he's a big mystery. And I'm not going to start an argument with anyone, but I probably know the most about him, which is absolutely nothing.

The kid doesn't show up for school until the second week and when he does, does he cause a stampede. He towers over everyone, the biggest kid in town. I find out his name is Ring Maxwell.

It knocks me for a loop when I find out that he is in the same grade as me, and when kids start making remarks about a big klutz like him being in the sixth grade, he informs them he is exactly eleven years and ninety days old, in a voice as rough and deep as John Travolta's. That makes them back away.

I'd just like to tell him that I'm eleven years and one hundred and seventy-five days old and that size doesn't count. But at first he doesn't want to talk to me. He's always slipping past me around the corners like he never saw me before. I guess he is embarrassed about the swans attacking him.

But I have a good reason for wanting to get hold of him. I am still wearing my cruddy shoes from that day at the cemetery, mud stains and all. I don't want to suck up to him; I just want to get my hands on him.

After cracking my elbow a few times going around a door fast trying to catch him, I finally corner the kid at the end of the hall, slouching along, pretending he doesn't see me.

"Hey, man!" I yell at him loud enough so everyone up and down the hall can hear me.

"Hey, man!" His voice cracks, going from high to high C.

"See any big birds lately?"

I'd be a liar if I didn't say I shrunk that kid right down to size, at least for a few seconds. He tries to stare me down, eye to eye.

I start pumping my elbows up and down like wings and twisting and stretching out my neck like a wild goose, squawking loudly.

Then suddenly he lets out a scream louder than my squawking, and he doubles over laughing. And he can't stop. He's out of control.

I stand there like a dummy for a minute. I hadn't intended to make him happy. But I feel it swelling up in my belly like I'm going to explode. I've got to either scream or laugh.

Well, after that it seems every time I turn around I bump into him, and without me even asking him he starts walking home from school with me.

Chapter 3

For a while I don't invite him in. I yell good-bye
and run up the walk and bang the door behind
me. Then, like a sneak, I peek out the curtain to
watch him leave. But he just stands there staring
at our house for a minute before he walks away. It
makes me feel as bad as leaving a dog out in the
snow.

I have my reasons and it's a lot of things. First
of all, we live in a real dump with a big old porch
tacked on, and it hasn't been painted in twenty
years. Inside it is so stuffed with Mattie's plants,
you can't find a place to walk. Geraniums in the
windows and on the floor and two cacti as big as
trees.

On her bad days Kate says we live in squalor. "Not quite," I always tell her. "Look at the ceilings, high enough to fly a plane through, and a kitchen the size of a skating rink. How many have that?"

"As if we needed a rink. And cold as a glacier in the winter," she says.

Anyway, I like to imagine our house was an old stagecoach stop with a romantic history. I tell quite a few lies to that affect to Ring. Mattie brags she was born here and that Kate was born here, too. That was enough for me. So I add to my lies. I tell Ring that our old family place was handed down from one member to another, going back to Columbus's time.

Ring acts impressed. So one afternoon I say, "Why don't you come in."

It's too bad I waited. Nothing seemed to bother him. Mattie greets us at the door, and she might make anyone take a second look, little as a ten-year-old kid and her wild hair piled on top of her head. She stands on her tiptoes and peeks at him from behind her hand, and then she leans back to see him better, like she's looking up at our water tower.

"Kind of puny, isn't he?" Mattie's got the idea she really is a clown.

She is one to take you by the chin in a firm grip and pull your head down so you're looking her straight in the eyes when she's talking to you. Ring is so tall she grabs me instead and calls me Lucas. I glance over at Ring. Some days it could be she doesn't remember. Sometime she acts like she has three sails to the wind. The doctor says Mattie functions like someone after three martinis—old age with complications.

I push her hand away. "My name is Ben! I keep telling you. Ben! Short for Benjamin Franklin, the smartest man ever born."

Kate told me this noble fact along with the truth that Lucas was my uncle and that he is dead and has been for ten years. "Thickheaded as they come, and a drunk to boot! Anyway, you're no Lucas," she said.

It depresses the heck out of me to be called Lucas.

But my point is, Ring stands there smiling like this is a very interesting place, and he is pleased with everything he sees, including Mattie. Even when she talks about the president visiting with her on our front porch or grandpa coming for an evening stroll. He's been dead twenty years.

Don't feel sorry that I am talking this way about Mattie, and I'm not a smart-ass, either. I can remember when she was younger and she had a tongue like a rattlesnake, a real sharpie. She could make me laugh while she took my hide off.

But now she is doing freaky things like telling Ring about her million dollars coming in the mail. The amazing thing is, he joins right in.

"The letter says I am a winner!"

"You'll probably get a telephone call, too," Ring says.

"No, the mail." Mattie shakes her head. "It always comes in the mail."

"I would say it'll be delivered." Ring has his head cocked, and his brow wrinkles in serious study. "You know, a million dollars is a lot."

"The mail," Mattie says.

I motion to Ring to follow me into the front room and then turn on the TV, but here is what is so funny. When Ring doesn't follow me, I peek back—there he is, still having a huge conversation with Mattie.

"Yup," he says, "a lot of money. You can take a trip anywhere you want to go. By plane or train or boat."

Oh, man!

"Some day you can get a car for Ben," Ring says.

Mattie turns to me. "I think I'll take a trip first."

Ring nods his head. "Good idea. I'll go with you. To Chicago."

"They have a zoo there."

I start to laugh; I can't hold back anymore. But when I take a look at Ring he isn't laughing. He shakes his head at me in a disgusted way, and he goes on talking with Mattie.

Chapter 4

With Ring on my heels I go out to the kitchen to put on the tea water. That is always the first thing that Kate asks for when she comes in the door.

Ring pitches right in without asking, and he helps me peel potatoes and fry hamburgers.

"You're really good," I tell him. "Your folks must run a McDonald's."

"Why?" He stops slicing potatoes and looks at me. "What did you say that for? It's none of your business what my folks do."

"Hey, I was only kidding."

"Oh yeah. Just kidding." He goes back to slicing potatoes.

Kate backs through the door with two sacks of groceries in her arms and kicks it shut. She walks past Ring without seeing him and puts the cereal and canned tuna in the cupboard and shoves the milk and meat in the fridge.

"Just leave me alone tonight," she says. She leans on the counter and stares into space. Her face is red from the September heat, and her hair is sticking to her forehead, and she has sawdust on one cheek. I'm used to Kate being the size of a chipmunk and wearing baggy pants and a turtleneck. I see Ring take a second look.

"Chow?" I say loudly, and clear my throat so she might notice we're not alone.

"Smells good. Where's Mattie?" She turns around and sees Ring. Nothing surprises her. She reaches for a cigarette, and Ring lights it for her before you can say bingo. I about fall over because Kate would have slapped my hand away.

"Thanks. Aren't you the gentleman," she says to Ring.

"I try."

"Relax," she says to me. "Who's your friend?" She can always read me like I came in big print.

"Ring. He's from school."

"I am Kate Gallegar." She holds out her hand.

Kate brushes sawdust out of her hair and flops into a chair while Ring and I set the table. I see him looking at her——little quick glances like he did with Mattie. She notices. "I make yo-yos in a toy factory. That's my job," she says kind of huffy.

Ring starts asking all kinds of questions about yo-yos, the same way he talked to Mattie about her million dollars. And Kate is very willing to talk. She tells Ring about her important boss, old Delaney with his Ph.D., who decided for the good of his soul—and to avoid a nervous break-down—that he needed to create something of substance and work with his hands as well as his brains.

I guess Ring must like the smell of hamburgers because he stays for supper. No one actually invites him, but he is kind of classy the way he handles things without making any waves. He sort of blends in so you forget he is there. One of us. That is one of his peculiar talents.

And I suppose that's the reason Kate talks to him like she's known him all her life. "Anyway," she says, "it affects me the same way as old Delaney, making those yo-yos. It's kind of uplift-ing and pleasant. Think of it—all those little kids bouncing those yo-yos. All that joy!" And Kate smiles like making toys is a spiritual trip to Disney World.

Mattie bangs on the table for attention. She

takes a piece of meat out of her mouth and jumps up. "You didn't call and say you were bringing me a piano, did you, Lucas?"

"Nope, and I'm not Lucas. Put your meat back in your mouth! You have a piano." I push her back in her chair.

Kate quits eating and I hear her taking deep breaths, which she usually does before she starts crying. She leans toward Ring. "She was a very dear mama when I was a little girl." Then Kate gets real agitated. "Those darn letters coming all the time, telling Mattie she is going to win a dozen mattresses, a trip to Hawaii, or maybe a Lincoln with a piano in it. It upsets her. Now everyone be quiet. You, too, Mattie."

But Mattie doesn't shut up. "I wonder who sent it." She raises her little hands and starts clawing the air like she's playing the piano. "I keep wondering what I want to play first when I get the piano."

Then Mattie laughs in a gay little way, and Kate laughs with her. She says, "Mattie, some day you're going to kill me."

Mattie puts her skinny little arms around Kate, and they lean their heads together.

I'd like to fall through a crack in the floor. But when I look over at Ring he has a soupy smile on his face.

"Okay, so she can play the piano. The one she wants to play, right here. Okay?" Kate shrugs and smiles. She points to the table. Her eyebrows drift up in a warning sign, meant for me. Then Kate waltzes her hands in the air, the same as Mattie, playing the same tune, I suppose.

"Good idea." Ring squats down beside Mattie, so darn polite and sincere. "Sounds good to me. It don't hurt none."

And the whole thing takes off with Ring leading us down a zany path like watching a movie run backward, which, of course, doesn't make any sense.

"What are you going to play first, Mattie?" And Ring is looking at her like he is expecting to hear some wonderful classical music the same as Liberace used to play.

"'A Red, Red Rose.'" Mattie puts her puckery face close to Ring's.

"That's no song." I tap her on the arm.

But she starts singing anyway, her voice cracking on the high notes:

O, my luve's like a red, red rose
That's newly sprung in June.
O, my luve's like the melody,
That's sweetly played in tune.

"I think that's a poem." Kate has her head cocked, tapping her foot, listening, with her face kind of puzzled. "Not a song, is it?"

With Ring squatting beside her, Mattie keeps humming to herself and pawing the air like the piano is in her lap. In a minute Ring joins in. His voice is higher pitched than Mattie's, and it cracks suddenly into a coarse burp.

In a minute Kate is humming, too, along with Mattie and Ring, all of them swaying back and forth in time. Just to be funny I start humming.

First thing I know I have let loose like somebody untied a rope around my chest, and I'm trying to sing louder than anybody. Me! A first-class schizo. Ring's got us all hypnotized.

Anyway, my teacher, Miss Bunn, was always telling me I was a messed-up kid. Introverted, she called it. She explained it meant looking inside my head too much, and I've got to stop, because my brain is shrinking up into a knot the size of a walnut. "It's worse than smoking," she warned. "Try to let yourself go sometimes."

I wonder what I would see if I looked inside Ring's head. He is like some sort of weird puzzle. For instance, tonight he is trying to move in like he is a member of our family, only he isn't. And tonight I got this warm feeling about him, like I have known Ring all my life, only I haven't.

Suddenly he looks at the clock and yells, "Jeez!" And he's out of there. When I try to walk with him he doesn't wait. He's going faster than speed.

In a minute I hear what sounds like the squawking of a Canadian goose, only it's Ring. That's the way it was with him: one minute Ring was there and the next minute Ring was gone.

Chapter 5

It is the second day after the picnic. Instead of running straight to the river, I go out past the old brick schoolhouse where Ring lives. I want to talk to Josie and Purcell, but I'm so nervous it makes me sweat. My stomach feels like someone poured lye in it. I run up the drive then turn around. I'm chicken. They might not want to talk to me about Ring.

I think about the first time I came out here. After Ring was at my house, he couldn't wait to take me home with him.

Quite a few people in town were surprised, and a few had a good laugh, when they heard that Ring's folks had rented the old brick school-house. It had been empty for ten years and was really run down. When I heard about it I wanted to laugh, too. I didn't, but I was just as curious.

It would have been hard to find if Ring hadn't been leading the way. You couldn't see it from the road. When we turn down the lane it is so over-grown with weeds, some as tall as I am. It is like a path through the jungle, and the old trees haven't been trimmed for years, the branches hanging down, slapping us in the face like an old wet mop. The old brick schoolhouse was sure hidden away.

Ring is really enjoying it, sometimes leading me off the path and hurrying ahead, then jump-ing out and surprising me, as if he is trying to shake me up or lose me.

We walk almost a block before we can see the school. It sits up on a little hill, two stories high, square, sticking above the trees, a fire escape down one side.

First of all, you can't tell anybody lives there, until you are walking through the door. I mean, Josie doesn't try to fool anyone about this being a schoolhouse. Outside the door is an old bell, long rope and all, still hanging. Of course, later on we have to ring it every time we go in and out. His mom doesn't care. She thinks it's a good joke.

But not Kate. She told me she could hear that

crazy bell as far away as the toy factory, which is plenty noisy. Of course, Kate raised her eyebrows like she is giving me two messages instead of one. "What kind of ding-a-lings need that kind of noise?" And the second message is, "And whoever heard of a doorbell with a rope?"

So I figure I'm not going to be surprised by anything else. But I am. First we go down a few steps to what he says is the first floor. It looks more like a basement to me. It has windows on every side that go right down to the ground.

He says, "This is my dad's studio where he paints. He is an artist." Ring says this very explicitly. "That's one reason we got this place—plenty of room."

Then he takes me upstairs to what I guess is the gym, only now it is their living room of sorts. There are a few big chairs and benches and tables with lamps. It is kind of empty, like the waiting room at the bus station, but there is a huge TV at one end of the room and a Ben Franklin stove in the corner.

At first I think it is loaded with windows on every side. Out one window I see streets and houses. I walk from one window to another. Another has a busy street, paved walks, and green grass. Then it dawns on me—we're in the middle of the woods. I want to hit myself in the head, jar my brains, because what I am looking at is real freaky; all those crazy windows with the fluffy curtains and the beautiful scenery of houses and yards and white picket fences are painted on the solid wall.

Ring is watching me. "Do you like it? Purcell did it. We needed windows, so he painted us some. Josie doesn't like blank walls. 'Pick what you want to see out your window,' Purcell said. What do you think?" Ring keeps looking at me.

I don't dare tell Ring what I think. He can make things sound so normal, like everybody does it.

He points at the basketball hoops at either end of the room, each filled with a pot of ivy that trails halfway to the floor. "Josie's idea of decorating."

I am busy trying to imagine running the length of this big room, dribbling a basketball around the furniture and shooting into a pot of ivy.

Anyway, I decide the whole thing is pretty neat. Then we go upstairs where there are two bedrooms off a balcony that overlooks the gym. Ring's room is like walking into bird land. The walls are covered with pictures of birds, from chickadees to pelicans. There is an old bird's nest coming apart on a shelf and all kinds of bird books: *Our Amazing Birds, Bird Ambulance, 1001, Questions About Birds.*

His remote-control boat and a set of binoculars are on another shelf above his bed. Then I look to see what Ring's view is out his window. I move closer because it sure surprises me—an ocean, just stretched out as far as I can see. Anyway, it seems that way, and there's a stone lighthouse with a light beaming out to sea and seagulls circling.

"He can really paint, can't he?" Ring nudges me from behind.

That's when I see something I hadn't noticed before. It is a little bird perched on Ring's bed, with bright blue feathers, its wings kind of spread as if it is going to fly. It looks so real, I touch it; the little bell on its neck squeaks.

Ring reaches around me and picks it up. "I don't want you touching that!" He puts it in a drawer of his chest. His face is red when he looks at me. "I've had it a long time. I don't want anyone touching it. It's old."

Suddenly I start getting the creeps, like nothing is real. It might all float away, like a surreal dream you see in the movies. It sure isn't like our house that feels and looks as if it had been planted there along with the oaks and the elms and might have roots to China.

But someone calls for Ring from downstairs. Ring drags me down there after him. Ring's mom, Josie, is standing at the bottom of the steps looking up at me. She is t-a-l-l. She doesn't say one word while I'm walking down, not until I am standing in front of her.

"Ben," she says.

I nod my head. My tongue feels glued to the top of my mouth.

"I'm Ring's mom. You can call me Josie." Her face has a funny curious look, like she is trying to read me the same as Kate is always doing. I feel her eyes kind of picking me apart.

I'm trying to think of a real smart reply. When someone puts something to you, you ought to say something back and not act stupid. "I'll bet you miss . . . " I trailed off. I don't know which place to mention, New York City or Cincinnati, Ohio, and I'm sure not going to say another planet.

"Oh, no." She shakes her head without mentioning where she might have come from or what she doesn't miss, just like Ring. She makes me nervous the way her eyes change—you know, how a cat's eyes change, getting bigger and the pupils darken, and they become quite dangerous looking.

Then she takes a big breath and she comes unwound. "It was nice to move here."The words came out with a big sigh of relief. "It's good to be here." She pauses, glancing over at Ring. Her eyes are kind of soft and moony now. "Isn't it, Ring? We like it, don't we?"

"Don't overreact." And that's how I meet Ring's dad. He walks up behind me, a guy with a shaggy beard and hair plastered flat to his head. His voice is kind of growly, and at first he scares the heck out of me. And then I think of all the windows he painted so they can look out, and I get to thinking how great that is.

I shake his hand and say, "Ben, here," and he says, "Purcell, here." He doesn't stay around and Josie just goes on talking.

"Ben," she says kind of quick and impatient, "how long have you lived here?" And her questions come faster than I can answer, all very personal.

"Your dad?"

"He's dead."

"Oh, I'm sorry. Your mother? Just the two of you?"

"No, there is Mattie." I don't explain her.

"Maybe I can meet your mother."

"She works."

Ring's mom sits there waiting for me to tell her more.

"She makes yo-yos." It always sounds so silly when I mention that. "Yo-yos," I repeat. "You throw them and they come back to you. She likes it. She says it is very pleasant work."

"It sounds interesting."

Ring is listening, too, like he's never heard the facts before, or else he's worried I'm not going to say the right sort of junk to impress his mom.

"We've not stayed very long in one place, have we?" She is looking at Ring. "We haven't been here too long, but maybe we'll stay. How about that, Ring?" She waits for him to answer.

"Sure." And they kind of lock eyes.

"Maybe." She reaches in her pocket and puts on her sunglasses, even though it is getting dark. And I know it is some sort of signal for me to go home.

Chapter 6

It's hard to remember how it really was. When I try to think of Ring it's blurred, mixed-up, like I'm as old as Mattie. Three days have passed and any news about him is on the TV, which isn't much. I don't turn it on. And now Kate leaves me alone.

At first Ring had a tough time at school, because he was such a funny big bugger. The kids didn't know how to handle him. He drove them crazy and they called him flaky. I guess it's because he acted like he was in a deep fog, thinking out loud and saying the screwiest things like he can prove the world is square. When anything happened that couldn't be explained, they'd swear he did it. They didn't take into consideration that he might be the smartest kid in school and smart enough not to let them know.

And Ring's so darn polite. You know, genuine, but it was one of the obstacles he had to overcome. Most kids want you to be as crummy as they are. Anyway, to begin with, some of them roughed him up and called him chicken neck. The thing is, they treated him like an outsider. And I could see that bothered him.

But then something strange happens. At first it starts slowly, then builds as the kids start to pay more attention to him. I don't think he even notices. You see, when he starts talking it is usually something out of the ordinary, something they don't know, haven't heard, or never guessed. Peculiar, like breaking into a zoo or sleeping up on the roof of a fifty-story building in a rainstorm.

And before you know it, Ring glows like he has flames shooting out his ears, a stupefied audience of kids hanging on to his every word. Eventually, it beings to affect Ring, and he is enjoying it as much as an old cat likes stretching out in the sun. His stories get wilder and wilder.

The strangest facts are about Ring's relatives,

starting with his cousins, Siamese twins joined at birth and, of course, separated later, who pretended to be sawed in half at a magic show. Ring says it was real dramatic when they showed their old scars where they had been separated.

Then there's this friend of his, a kid named Fox. When Ring talks about him it's like there must be a book the size of an encyclopedia written about him. He has a story for every day of the month. Some of them are funny stories, but some are sad, too. When Ring talks about him his eyes get kind of dreamy, squinty, like they are full of smoke. Especially when he talks about Fox curling up with a lion cub to keep warm or sleeping in a tree one night.

For instance, one afternoon walking home from school we are eating a Baby Ruth we split. Ring stops me in the middle of the street.

"How'd you like to eat a bushel of these? Eat all night until you heave?"

"Oh yeah."

"I mean it."

I give him a shove. "What do you think?"

"Well, one night Fox got locked in this Come-and-Go store."

"How?"

"On purpose."

"How come?"

"He was hungry."

"They kick him out?"

"They didn't know he was there. He hid in the storage room behind the freezer. As soon as they locked up he started eating—all night. Nothing but candy and pop and peanuts."

"What a life!"

"On an empty stomach."

"Who cares?"

Ring leans over and hugs his stomach like he's dying. He pretends to heave all over the sidewalk.

"They caught him?"

"Laying flat in front of the candy counter the next morning. They thought he was dead. They rushed him to the hospital and started pumping. For ten hours they pumped."

"Oh my gawd!"

Ring runs on ahead of me. He's laughing himself silly. "They really got him pumped out. Fox says he's missing his liver and a kidney."

"You lie!" I don't try to catch up with Ring. I let him go on ahead and I go home.

Chapter 7

I'm getting fidgety so I go out to the woods this afternoon, and I walk about a half mile along the river. I can't keep my mind off Ring and how long he's been gone. Four days tomorrow, only it seems like years.

And I can't seem to stop telling the stories that had come out of Ring's mouth. It worries me. It gets so I can really blow things up big about Fox. Like I know for sure it is true, like I know Fox.

But I don't know Fox, and I should quit telling Ring's crazy stories over and over. Kate says I'm beginning to sound loony. If I don't stop, she will take me to a head doctor. She said that not long after Ring walked into the river.

When Kate gets home from work tonight, she shakes her head first thing, which means no news about Ring, then I ask her, "Do you think Ring told me some really big ones—all that stuff he filled me up with about Fox?"

"You mean like the one about the kid having his stomach pumped for ten hours? Or sleeping in a tree all night? You'd have to be a little simple-minded to believe that."

Mattie laughs. "Okay, those stories plus a hundred other," I say.

"I'd say he had a good imagination."

"Does he think I'm dumb?"

"He thinks you are a friend. Someone to have fun with." Kate pats me on the shoulder.

"Sometimes it's like his mind goes in circles, just grabbing at everything."

"Doesn't hurt. Maybe he'll be a comic writer."

I watch Kate nibbling on her tuna sandwich and say, "You think maybe he is just a dreamer—a daydreamer like you?"

"I'm a dreamer? Okay, could be. What's the difference? A dream or the truth? Whatever makes you happy." She wrinkles her nose like she does to flip off the sawdust. "They can be the same, but they seldom are. One helps the other sometimes. A dream can help you blur the truth, rub it out."

"So who cares?" I suddenly want to quit thinking about it.

Mattie goes out to the porch and looks in the mailbox. When she comes back without a letter she is in a bad mood. Ring helped Mattie keep her crazy dreams alive, too. So I tell her the story about Fox curling up with the lion cub to keep warm. It makes her laugh and forget about the mail that she didn't get.

And Kate smiles in a dreamy sort of way. That is her problem, too. She daydreams about my dad. His picture is hanging on the wall in the front room. Sometimes when she stops and looks at him, she smiles like he's right there in the room.

It is his graduation picture. His hair is quite fuzzy and stands up. He is kind of homely and sweet looking, like Lyle Lovett. But sometimes when Kate looks at my dad, she gets a puzzled and hurt look.

"Oh, well," she says finally through a big sigh. Her face gets kind of soft, and she puts her hands on my face and pats my cheeks like she might be petting a puppy. She squints her eyes and stares at me.

"You're looking like your dad. Bet you'll be shaving in a year or two."

"I suppose. Ring is getting a lot of fuzz on his upper lip."

"You'll catch up with him."

Chapter 8

It rains all night. I hate the sound of the water coming down, but I get up early anyway. I sit on the damp steps like an idiot.

Some mornings Ring waited for me until I got up. I wondered if he had sat there all night.

He started coming earlier and earlier. One morning he was yelling outside my window at five o'clock. It was November and still dark.

Kate is yelling from her room. "Who's out there?"

"Someone for jogging?" Ring yells back.

"Hush up," Kate says, quieter. "It's still dark. You'll wake the neighbors up."

I'm not too excited to go jogging. I'd rather be

in bed. But anyway, we run all the way to school, then around the track. In a few days we start running on the road. He doesn't try to make it easy for me. In his loose free-wheeling way he runs as if someone is after him, at lightning speed. On my short legs is darn near impossible to keep up with him. Sometimes he runs ahead and hides from me.

One time we ran as far as the park. There's a big old swamp in there. But we don't go over the fence. That's good because old Meeker, our county conservation officer, is coming down the trail. He'd chase us out.

I really want Ring to see the swamp. It is so weird in the half dark of dawn. We walk along the fence to get a closer look. Ring acts like we've discovered America before Columbus— the black water, and the dead trees like skeletons and the sounds wild and unknown are giving him a real thrill.

But I don't tell him what old Meeker said about the swamp, as he told me to keep my mouth shut, or else. And for a guy as crazy about birds as Ring is, with all his bird books and his binoculars, it is going to knock him off his toot if I ever do tell him.

Well, anyway, we'd been running a couple of weeks, when one morning, for no reason, he just starts screaming. The sound is worse than our noon whistle. It near blows my eardrums.

When he stops long enough for me to ask why he is screaming that way, he says, "So someone will know I'm alive." He lets out another scream.

"I know."

"Not you."

I go down the list, starting with Mattie and his folks, but he stops me.

"Not them! Not anyone you know. Forget it!" He runs on ahead of me, then he waits for me to catch up. He starts telling me about Fox living in Lincoln Park in the middle of Peoria.

"Fox ran to get warm first thing in the morning when he slept there. And it helped him to scream, too," Ring says. "It feels good. It helps to unstring me."

So every morning Ring and I scream as loudly as we can when we get out of town far enough. Once in a while Ring throws in a few bird squawks. I get to enjoying it. I really feel leveled out by the time I get to school.

But the screaming stops fast. One morning a police car comes whizzing by, and the cops turn on their siren. The guys wave and go on, just some of their horseplay. But it scares the spit out of Ring. So we go back to running around the track with our mouths shut.

It is starting to rain again, and the seat of my pants are already soaked through from the wet steps. Kate yells for me to come in and eat breakfast.

Chapter 9

In the afternoon when it quits raining I take a walk toward Ring's place, but when I get to the drive I don't have nerve enough to go in.

It's been four days and I haven't seen his folks. I don't know if they want to see me. I don't know what to do. So I go to places where Ring and I went, down back roads and along the swamp. I look every place we used to go. When I get home I find a note from Josie: *Sorry we missed you*. I can't believe I missed them.

Kate says, "Oh, Ben, it's a shame you didn't stay home."

Kate was always curious about them, Josie and Purcell. One night when I first knew Ring, she said, "How come we never see his folks around town? Such spooky people."

"How'd I know?"

"I don't think she ever shops in a grocery store. Not once have I seen her. No wonder Ring is so skinny."

"Oh brother, don't worry. I know what he eats is better than tuna casserole." Kate's idea of a banquet.

"What about him, the dad?"

"He's on the road. Maybe he buys his razors in Chicago."

"Well, maybe she buys her groceries in Chicago, too," Kate snapped.

But when Josie suddenly crawls out of her cocoon and we start seeing her around town, she has a very good reason. To begin with, it's like she's been sampling our town in small bites, the library and the telephone company first. But the main reason is to hear Ring debate.

Ring is turning out to be quite a brain. Josie swells up over his standardized test scores. It's the only way he can get into school until his records arrive. Because he'd been home schooled, Josie says. In just three months he is moved ahead a grade, and all that junk.

And, of course, he is good at talking, arguing especially, so he's a natural for debates. He has favorite subjects. Rights! Kids' Rights! Dogs'

Rights! Anybody's Rights! He gets real serious and mad acting when he debates in class.

So in middle school he gets to debate a lot. The first time, he argues that people should be able to keep chickens and a cow in town, if they need the food. After he wins, he surprises everyone by sneaking a chicken into his locker and running down the hall with it squawking its head off, until they both get kicked out.

Anyway, he wins every debate, sometimes against the high school kids. I tell Kate he can grab ideas out of the air and then talk about them so fast you can't keep up.

So Ring gets the honor of debating before the school board with the high school team on an important subject, especially for the kids. The question: Should a wing be added to Green Hills High School?

It turns out it is only practice before the team competes with another school. But the teacher makes it very important, putting the team up on the stage in the gym. And of course, they have folding chairs lined up across the floor, like a million people are going to be there.

I don't see Josie until they are ready to start, and I notice Purcell slip in later and stand at the back. Ring must have seen them, too, because he looks pleased, and he doesn't look scared, just quiet, waiting to chew up the negative speaker.

But no one explains to the kids beforehand that in order to add on a new wing they'd have to dig up the football field, which would have made a big difference to Ring.

I guess it's a case of Ring outsmarting himself. He not only wins the debate, he's so convincing that the school board seriously starts thinking about putting on a new wing. Of course, that makes all the kids mad at him, and I tell him to stay away from the football team for his health's sake.

But the rest of the town is treating Ring like a hero. And the funny thing is most everyone agrees the school needs a new wing. And Ring says his folks come to quite a few things at school now.

"Maybe after a while they won't stick out like sore thumbs," Kate says.

Chapter 10

It starts to rain again, and after I go to bed a wind comes up, a real zinger, and it sets up a howling in our rainspouts. A murmuring, Mattie calls it. And it makes me think of last Christmas when I almost got blown away walking out to Ring's. Which is actually something I'd like to forget.

The day before Christmas, Ring's mom calls and invites us for Christmas dinner, and Kate says we can't go.

Her excuse is Mattie can't go anyplace to eat because of the way she spits out her food.

"It's you, you don't want to go," I tell her when she gets off the phone.

"Oh, bull," she says.

"I think it's you."

"Do you want me to go trotting over there in my underwear and the only thing new I've got to wear, and my old bedroom slippers?"

I am too mad to laugh at her.

And Kate has to mention that she doesn't know Josie from a hole in the ground. "And all the strange things they do! Painting windows on their walls and living in a schoolhouse." Some of the things I told Kate when I should have kept my mouth shut.

But it is upsetting to Ring. He comes over in the afternoon to convince Kate. He's really trying to soft-soap her into coming, asking her a zillion questions about making yo-yos, even though she's probably already told him every piece of yo-yo information she knew. But it'd be easier to talk to a post, as far as Kate listening. Next he works on Mattie, talking about the trip they are going to take.

Then he turns to me. "And I thought you'd come for sure." But the whole point is, we are letting him down—he calls it a terrible disappointment.

At times I can make Ring laugh when I do something so dumb it's disgusting. I think it's one of the reasons he likes me. Now I can't make him laugh. He's like a guy working on something that is a deep secret. I get funny little hints bubbling up between us.

When he starts home I walk partway with him. I tell him about Kate and Mattie dancing around our skinny Christmas tree to "Hark, the Herald Angels Sing."

"You should see them. They kept perfect time. Mattie keeps her eyes closed and a big smile on her face, just waltzing and humming away, like a little kid."

It doesn't make him laugh. "Forget it. I don't like Christmas music or Christmas jokes, like everyone is so happy. Maybe they really aren't." I give him a look, but he doesn't say anything else.

Before I start home I tell Ring I will come over Christmas afternoon. But the first thing early in the morning I get a call.

"Don't come over. I won't be home. See you around." He's quiet a minute, then he adds, "Keep your nose clean. I'll see you in a few days."

"My nose is clean," I yell. He is already gone.

Kate is listening. "Now what?"

I repeat what Ring said. "'Don't come over. I won't be home.'"

"Come again?" Kate stand in front of me with her hands on her hips.

"That's what he said," I glare at her.

"I suppose it's my fault."

"Well. You wouldn't go to his house."

"That's really a switch. It's a good thing we weren't planning to go over there to eat! No one home!"

"They must have changed their minds." I'd like to kick Ring in the butt, and I don't need Kate yelling at me, too.

Mattie pulls an ornament off the Christmas tree and puts it in her hair. It makes Kate laugh, and she brings a pile of packages to the middle of the table, like we do every Christmas. Kate pours me coffee and pushes a plate of doughnuts my way. And we open presents.

Guess what? Jeans and a sweatshirt and a geeky shirt with a collar. Mattie does a dance for us with her new scarf wrapped around her waist. And, of course, Kate acts overcome when she sees her present from me: a box of bath powder and a tiny bottle of perfume that goes with it. We have to hide Mattie's Christmas candy so she won't eat it all for breakfast.

Later when it snows outside the house starts

filling up with chicken and pumpkin pie smells, and Kate has Christmas music on the radio so loud, it is rattling our windows. I quit worrying so much about Ring. Meeker turns up to eat chicken with us. Kate justifies inviting him by calling him "that lonely fellow." Anyway, he's got a corny sense of humor, and he keeps us laughing, especially Mattie.

But later in the afternoon I start thinking about that crazy Ring again and start losing my cool. The main thing I've got to find out is whether he's lying to me.

It is a crazy idea. The wind is blowing the snow around, almost a howling blizzard making the icy weeds crackle and thrash around on the path. Mattie used to tell me when we heard the wind blowing hard it was like the murmur of the crowd who followed Jesus, and today that makes my skin crawl.

I can't see any footprints or tracks of any kind in the snow around the brick schoolhouse, just tracks leading down the drive. First I pull the frozen rope on the doorbell. But despite all the clanging there is no answer. Next I run around the school trying to see into the studio through the ground windows. I can't see anything. The only things that look alive are the trees doing some kind of step and shuffle in the wind.

By the time I start home I'm half frozen. My teeth are chattering. Kate says I must have the flu. She shoves me off to bed early and comes in later and covers me so tight that I can't move. She puts an ice pack on my forehead. She says I am hot enough to heat water for tea. For three days she keeps me in bed. She says several times, "This is a lovely way to spend your Christmas vacation." But at least she doesn't mention Ring.

Once in a while I think I might be willing to listen to one of Ring's unbelievable stories to pass the time. On the fourth morning I hear Kate bang the front door and come rushing up to my room. She throws a card onto my bed. It is from Chicago. It shows a chubby little kid in a nightgown aiming a bow and arrow at an old wobbly guy with a cane and a long beard. Underneath it says: *Your time has run out. Happy New Year.* It is signed *Guess who?* A dumb joke and I don't feel much like laughing. So he went to Chicago. So what?

He comes by on New Year's Eve acting like he's never been gone, acting disgustingly cheerful. He brings chocolates for Mattie and Kate and two books for me, ones he had, he says, *Hatchet* and *Dogsong* by Gary Paulsen. Of course, Ring wants to know what I was doing while he was gone. I try to make having roast chicken with Kate and Meeker and Mattie sound like mountains of fun.

I'm not in the mood to deal with him. I look at *Dogsong* and take it to the bathroom with me and stay in there for about twenty minutes. When I come back he is in the middle of a story about his uncle Boyd, a relative he has never mentioned before. And as it turns out, his uncle Boyd is a social worker who lives in a walk-up apartment, six flights up, with his wife, Bessie, and her six cats and his dog, part German shepherd, big as a horse. And all they ate was Chicken Delight, and they drank Dr Pepper, even the cats and the dog. "The water could poison you," Ring says.

His laugh is too high and his eyes skip around the room, not settling on me too long. "They live in Chicago." His voice goes up, like it is a big question. Then he starts talking again about the German shepherd that's as big as a horse.

I interrupt him. "I went over to your house. I didn't think you'd be gone."

"A dog that big in an apartment!" He stops

talking suddenly. "You think I lied?" He looks hurt. "I told you I'd be gone."

"I know."

"It was something . . . " He has a hard time finding the right word. "We had to go," he says as he finally looks me straight in the eyes. "All of a sudden-like."

Then he is off talking to Kate who is busy stuffing chocolates in her mouth, listening as he describes his favorite book, *Jonathan Livingston Seagull*. You know it would have to be about a bird.

"I really get a kick out of a bird like that," he says. He keeps looking over at me.

"It can talk and think, and he is smarter than most of us figuring out things." Ring is talking louder. "The gull sees farthest who flies highest."

Mattie starts flapping her arms and mimics Ring, "The gull who flies highest . . . "

Ring puts out his arms and starts flapping around the room, too, his elbows whipping up and down. Like me in the hall that day. I'd like to slug him, but he's just too funny looking. Then he gives me a bear hug, really pins me and almost knocks me down. Then he wrestles me to the floor, and we roll all over the place with Mattie yelling and trying to get between us.

Anyway, things get settled down again. Mattie thinks she kept us from killing each other.

The trouble is, when I try to remember about last Christmas it is like I missed something Ring was trying to tell me. When I wake up in the night I think I hear Ring talking. "I swear that's the truth," he is saying. I stare into the dark trying to see him, and then I know I've been dreaming again.

Chapter 11

This morning I can't go to the river. I just can't, so I walk across town to our school. I picture Ring going like a rabbit out ahead of me, like he always did. He hated the cold; it always made him run fast. He stopped at our house every day on the way home from school to get warm.

But on the coldest day last winter, in February on a Saturday afternoon, who should be pounding on our door? When Kate opened it there was Josie, a big, woolly head scarf covering most of her face, sunglasses, and only a speck of her chin peeking out at us. Ring was standing there next to her like he was frozen. It seemed like five minutes before Kate opened her mouth to say a few words like, "Hello . . . come in." I was embarrassed.

But Josie doesn't seem to notice and pushes Ring in ahead of her through the door. "It's colder than Hades out here, if you'll excuse me." She has her arms full of magazines. She drops them on the floor in one big bang where Kate points. She looks at Kate. "I'm Josie Maxwell."

Of course, Kate is in her usual T-shirt and grubby jeans, and barefoot as well. She has feet tough as a goat's. She really has to crack her neck to look at Josie.

It gets kind of quiet while Josie and Kate are sizing up each other. Ring is babbling a Fox story about how to sell a magazine. "When you get your foot in the door you sit down on the first chair," which Ring is doing. "It's hard to get rid of anyone glued to a chair. Hand the lady of the house the magazine opened to a glitzy page."

But the look on Ring's face is something else, kind of soupy and satisfied as he looks around at us fondly. Like, for instance, maybe we are his long-lost cousins, or maybe we came from the same neighborhood, the one you can see out the painted windows.

Mattie disappears from the room and comes

back with five empty cups and a tea bag hanging from each handle. When Kate notices, she jumps up and rushes to the kitchen, and a few minutes later she comes back with boiling water and fills each cup.

The moment Josie starts sipping her tea she starts talking. "Ring wanted me to come and see you."

Kate smooths her hair down, which is good. She tucks her bare feet under her chair. She appears to be tongue-tied. She looks at me and says, "Ring is a good kid."

"I like Ring," Mattie says.

"Sure do," I say, having to get in on the conversation someway.

Kate has such a pained look on her face that Ring keeps pushing the conversation along, furnishing a word here and there in an empty space. That is, until yo-yos are mentioned.

Josie only has to ask one question about yo-yos and it seemed to lift the burden from Kate. At first she looks at her hands as she talks. "We mostly put things together, especially yo-yos. Kids are crazy about them. Wooden toys of all kinds."

"I couldn't do that. No talent."

"You might be surprised. It isn't that hard."

"It must give you a good feeling."

Kate sighs. "I have time to think." She brushes her hair with her fingers like she does to get sawdust out. "The toys I make are kind of cute, you know. I can always see the kids playing with those yo-yos. Did you ever try it?"

And suddenly, like two old friends, Kate and Josie are huddled together. Then I realize I've never seen Kate like that—with a friend. I feel myself go limp with relief.

Ring is laying flat on the floor showing Mattie how to stack dominoes to fall properly and he is telling her about the kid who arranged three hundred thousand dominoes and what a brilliant engineering feat it was to be able to control how they would fall. "Fox could do it if he had the dominoes," he says. "I think maybe he has done it."

"So much for Fox," I say. Which shows I was starting to get jealous.

I hear Kate laughing, and Josie is telling her about the curious people coming in a stream like a colony of ants that just discovered sugar, to get a good look at their old brick schoolhouse. "Some days it really gives me a headache," she says. "But it was nice to move here."

"Some night I'm going to ring the school bell all night and wake up the town," Ring says, interrupting his mother. "Just watch."

Ring still has his punchy look, like he's been on a Ferris wheel all afternoon. Mattie tells Josie about the million dollars she is getting and the trip she is going to take with Ring to see the Statue of Liberty. Mattie reminds him again when they are leaving, "I want to see the Statue of Liberty, Ring. Don't forget!"

Going out of the door Josie pauses as if she is doing some deep thinking. She turns and looks at me so straight, then pats me on the shoulder. "You're good support for Ring."

When they leave it is like the wind dying, it is so quiet. Kate stands in the middle of the front room looking at all the plants, the pots of geraniums and the cacti, and the piano. She has a peculiar, studying look, then she makes a horrible face.

A little later she says, "I can't figure her. There is something fishy. Really fishy. But I like her." Kate pauses, and adds. "She likes me." Then she asks, "His dad?"

"He's an artist sometimes."

"That figures. What's he doing now?"

"He drives a tour bus. I already told you. He's gone a lot."

"That figures, too. She's lonely. I can tell."

In the next couple of weeks Kate tries to read the magazine Josie brought—*Harper's* and *Esquire* and *Atlantic Monthly*. "Not my style," she says, and she throws them all away. Mattie gathers them up and piles them in a corner of her room. She spends hours looking at the travel ads and the pictures of wine.

Whenever Ring comes over she tells him about the trips she will take, to Iceland, maybe Brazil, and Galveston, Texas. She hints about the Wild Turkey bourbon she has hidden under her bed. Ring pats her hand and listens very seriously.

Chapter 12

It's really early when I get to the school. I start circling the grounds, and I go out behind to watch the men putting up the wall for the new wing. It's blistering hot in the sun, but old Ring would sure get a kick out of this.

It was last March when they started it. One afternoon when I came out of school I heard a terrible rumbling out behind. I had to go and look. A big machine, the size of a dinosaur, was chewing away at our football field, the ground coming up in big chunks like a monster eating chocolate, and I felt big chunks coming up in my throat. It was the saddest thing I ever saw, all started by Ring's debate.

Ever since I was a little kid I planned on play-ing football once I weighed over a hundred pounds. There was still a chance I'd get there!

I jumped on the closest pile of dirt, frozen hard as a cake of ice, and I began to yell.

It is between snowing and sleeting, a rotten time to start digging a hole. Ring comes looking for me. We pull our caps to our noses, and shove the rest of our faces into our coat collars. We don't talk. We stand there watching like two wooden dummies. It looks like a grave being dug. Ring is kind of low, like he committed a crime. I don't try to cheer him up. Before we leave he says, "A bad mistake." I don't disagree.

On the way home he wants to stop at Wilke's Grocery. He has a hard time remembering it is a loaf of bread he came in for. We take a tour through the dairy department, and he has to look at the cheese, picking up a package and looking at it. Before we leave he buys a Baby Ruth candy bar, and he forgets the bread. That's when I first notice Ring acting kind of restless—picking things up and putting them down.

Next week it's the same thing. After school we go out and look at the hole behind the school, then he wants to stop at the Serve U Grocery.

And we wander around until we get to the cheese again. Then we walk on to the milk department, and Ring leans over and looks at every carton. A different kid is on each one— missing kids.

We have another blizzard, and we don't go back to a store for a couple of weeks. But then we have this nice day and the sun comes out, and the melting snow practically drowns us when we try to cross the street. And Ring has got the urge again. He insists we stop in Wilke's Grocery to buy us each a candy bar.

After he buys two Baby Ruths he goes back to the cheese and milk, and he strolls along looking at the cheese. Then he squats down and looks at the milk, like he's having a hard time deciding between one-percent and two-percent milk, only he's looking at the kids' pictures again.

Before we leave the store he goes over to the produce section, and he picks up a couple of apples and he sniffs a lemon. He's starting to make me nervous. He grins at me, his brows arched like a butterfly's wings. Then I know he's trying to get me excited. He motions toward his pocket and laughs out loud. I am beginning to get the drift.

It's one of Ring's favorite stories, about Fox and the fruit freak. Fox read about it in the *Inquirer*. How this guy held up stores and all he took was fruit. He held up about a hundred stores and he never got caught. So Fox tried it a few times, a banana or an apple, but once he grabbed a pineapple and tried to stuff it in his pocket. He got caught.

With all our horsing around, it was late when we start for home.

Ring was the first one to notice. We were turning the corner. "Hey, no lights in your house!"

"How come?" I ask a dumb question. I start running. I don't exactly panic. But all of a sudden my brain feels like a sponge. My house is dark. Not a spark of light. Mattie!

I open the door and call out kind of quiet. Then we both stop breathing and listen. Ring turns on the lights. The water is running in the sink, and the teakettle goes *ping*, dry as a bone and starting to smell. I grab it and shut the stove off. I crawl around on the floor and look under the table and in the broom closet.

"Ben!" Ring screams. He is holding Mattie's old blue coat and her woolly scarf. "She isn't in the house!" I think I almost faint. "It's freezing outside." Ring rolls up her coat in a ball and hands me the afghan off the davenport. He gives me a shove that gets me out the door and halfway to the street. "We'll go in opposite directions."

I run up driveways and peek in garages. But I'm just drifting. I can't get one thought to stick in my head except that Kate is going to kill me. It's a bad time enough for her; Kate always drags around all month. My dad died in March, and according to Miss Bunn, Julius Caesar got bumped off this month, and the Ides of March is a very sad day.

My hands ache from the cold because I left my mittens home. I put the afghan over my head and around my shoulders and wrap my hands in it. I get to the corner just as a bus pulls up. Kate isn't on it. But I give everyone on the bus a good laugh.

We find Mattie sitting on a park bench. No coat, no hat, all sprawled out like she is sunning herself, only it's dark.

"Mattie." Ring's voice sounds croaky and scared, it's so soft.

"We've been looking for you," I shout. She pays no attention to me. "Mattie!" I try again. "There aren't any ducks anymore!" She used to come here to see them. "What's the matter?" I yell to make me feel better, and I want to wake her up.

She just folds up then. We both grab, trying to pick her up, trying to push the other away, both of us tugging and hanging on to her and Mattie begins screeching like the devil's got her. Ring tears the afghan off me and wraps it around her.

"Who are you? I'll have you arrested," she keeps yelling at me. All the way home she yells she's being kidnapped.

When we get home Kate is there. She looks Mattie over good and gives her a cup of hot tea and tells her to shush, she isn't being kidnapped.

Ring sits down close beside her, studying her like he does when he thinks she is sad or upset. He talks about her million dollars and about their trip to New York to see the Statue of Liberty. He has Mattie laughing again, and she puts her hand in his.

"You could get lost, and no one would find you," I hear him say to her.

I'm feeling a heck of a lot better. When Ring starts for home I tag along with him for a few blocks. We run, bumping into each other and laughing like two goons, we're so relieved. The air is as cold as ice chips against my face. I feel good, especially about finding Mattie before she got hurt and staying out of trouble with Kate.

Ring stops once, long enough to say, "Hey, did you know you can tell time by the stars? Just look."

"What do you look for?"

"The hour hand, dummy."

"What time is it, then?"

He doesn't answer. He starts running so fast, I can't keep up with him. Once when he slows down I can hear him say, "It's the same as happened to Mattie. Fox lost his mom, too. And they never did see her again."

"Jeez!"

Then he puts his arms out like wings on a plane, and he tilts them just so, and he runs without any kind of bouncing up and down, really smooth.

When we get to the corner Ring says good-bye and gives me a high five and cuts through the park. I am just turning the corner when I hear him yelling. I look back and he is waving both arms.

"Ben, do you hear me? I think I'm going to learn to fly next year. I like it." His voice is squeaky high. "One of those twin-engine Cessnas. Look!"

And he puts out his arms like wings on a plane again, and he tilts them just so, and he runs without any kind of bouncing up and down. He keeps running as far as I can see. I can't stop watching.

The moon is shining off the snow, giving it a pinkish color that makes everything kind of eerie, like looking through a fog with a special light or like a lamp shining through the clouds.

Then all I can see is a shadow, like a plane coming in for a landing. I get goose bumps. I can hear Ring laughing from across the park. Then he fades away out of sight in the shadows, like he is taking off again.

"Jeez! I think I'll be a pilot," I yell.

I can hear Ring's laugh trailing out over the park. He is going faster, and the sound—like a plane going away higher and higher—the sound gets fainter and fainter until I can't hear him any longer.

I never felt like this before, looking up at the sky and thinking maybe I can fly, too.

Chapter 13

Sometimes Kate brings home news she hears at work about Ring, which is the same as no news. Most times I won't listen. I run out of the house. That's the trouble. I run away from everything, turn my brain off so I won't worry.

One night when she comes in from work she says, "You know, they have dragged the river to where it gets so narrow a cat can't squeeze through, not even deep enough for it to drown. For almost a week people have walked for miles through all the woods and weeds and poison ivy. I tried to talk to his mom. She doesn't have much to say. She's pale as a ghost, looks worried sick."

I run out to the brick schoolhouse almost

every day, but I never yank the rope to ring the bell. Sometimes I see Josie working hard in her garden, digging and shoveling like a madwoman. I always wave, but I don't stop. I don't know what to say to her. It doesn't seem like it's been almost a week since the picnic. Ring said it was going to be a real whoopee affair with both of our families. Did he mean to say good-bye?

I have to push myself to go over to the river this morning. I run along the bank looking in. I follow it for a few blocks, then I cut through, near the swamp where Ring went looking for birds.

He's a ring-a-ding about birds. I start laughing and I keep saying, "ring-a-ding." I like the sound of the words, and I get to laughing until I'm almost out of it, almost having a nervous breakdown over Ring and his birds. But still. I like saying it, "Ring-a-ding Ring."

Once he showed me his records that he kept of every bird that he ever saw, including a white owl, a loon, a pileated woodpecker, and a few that sound as if he made them up. He could spout bird facts at a dizzying rate, how they fly on perfectly designed wings, riding on updrafts, soaring. Then, on the first warm day last April, during Easter vacation, we walked a mile along the edge of the swamp.

Ring has his binoculars up to his eyes, stumbling along, not knowing where he is going, raving about all the birds that are back. The sky has turned as frosty as a glass of ice water, and the dry leaves from last fall crunch like glass under our feet. Ring has a fit every time I make a noise and scare a bird away. A crowd of starlings seems to be lost and lands in the tree in front of us.

Ring begins to name the birds. "Song sparrow."

"I know that."

"White-crowned sparrow."

"Yeah."

"Titmouse."

"Watch your mouth!"

"Finch."

Before he can name another bird I start yelling. "Blackbird! Blackbird! Blackbird!"

"Okay, okay," he says.

But I can't calm down. I'm excited because I know something about this swamp that would blow Ring away. But it's a deep secret, and I'm not supposed to breathe a word about it or I might get thumped on the head, sent out of the country. Anyway, that's what the conservation officer, Meeker, the friend of Kate's, said a few years ago when he told me. So it was what I considered an official secret. He caught me on the wrong side of the fence in the swamp. Where you are not supposed to go, the sign says.

And then Meeker told me why, and it would surprise a lot of people in Green Hills. Migrating whooping cranes stop in the swamp in back of the park every April and October. "Nobody in town knows it," he said. "We gotta protect them!"

Then he clamped his hand on my shoulder, so I know how important it is. Anyway, he swore me to secrecy to my dying day, and he said further that if a whooping crane was ever hurt back there in the swamp, he would hold me responsible. That was when he thumped me on the head and stared real hard into my face.

For two years I sneaked over the fence into the swamp whenever I dared. But I never found the whooping cranes, and I was beginning to think Meeker was a liar.

So that day I show Ring where to get over the fence into the swamp. We both get soaked, our pants wet to our knees from the deep grass and the mud sucking away at our shoes. Above us are more birds. About a million singing. Ring is busy pointing out a bunch of little ones, "Warblers," he calls them.

But it is beginning to bore the heck out of me. I was hoping that we might just happen to see those crazy whooping cranes and I can surprise Ring. We walk deeper into the swamp where there is a lot of water, little pools we have to jump over to get to a dry spot.

So I'm standing there trying to decide which way to jump, and I'm yacking away, and all of a sudden Ring grabs me and sticks his fist halfway down my throat.

Right in front of us are two whooping cranes wading in a little pool of water. They are the tallest birds I have ever seen, big as a man, kind of barefaced, with long skinny necks and a blotch of red on the top of their heads like they had been hit with a club.

If you want to know the truth, I'm so excited, I have trouble breathing. Ring doesn't make a sound. His face looks turned inside out surprised, showing all of his feelings.

Suddenly the largest whooping crane lowers its head and spreads its wings so you can see the black tips, and then it dips down and silently begins to whirl and leap and bow its head.

"My gawd! I think it's dancing," I whisper. It is about as funny as anything I'd ever seen. "Hey. Hey." My voice is croaky. The other crane leaps in the air and bends almost double. It's something I can't believe. It's like they must have practiced a couple of hours a day for a year, it is so perfect.

Ring doesn't say anything at first. I know this big bird is going on his list. Then I hear him letting out his breath, and he says, "Cool! Yeah!" Then just as quick he's quiet, and he puts his hand over my mouth again.

It really leaves me kind of paralyzed for a minute, and Ring, too. Then he hugs me so tight, I can hardly breathe. I hug him back. I feel like an electric current has passed through me and shocks Ring, because we start jumping up and down together.

When the whooping cranes move, we find a nice high spot, dry as a bun. Ring has turned serious now, and it is quiet and peaceful. I can hear my heartbeat echoing in my ears so loud, I worry that I might have a medical problem.

"It's something I wanted to show you," I say, feeling superior, because I have waited a long time for this.

Ring squeezes my arm, and I know I'm supposed to shut up. I hold my breath until I'm about ready to pop. "We're seeing something we're not supposed to see, the way Meeker tells it," I whisper. "They don't usually come this way."

"It's a crime, you know. If someone hurt a whooping crane, really was mean enough to shoot it . . ."

When it starts to get cool we crawl under some bushes. After a while my enthusiasm for cranes is fading, mainly because of all the darn gnats biting me.

Not Ring. He aims his binoculars at the sky where clouds of birds are coming over the swamp.

And then *bang*, he punches me in the ribs. We see a whole bunch of whooping cranes coming. They glide down into the wet grass, their wings outstretched, their legs like stick rudders; their necks laid out straight ahead. They come so fast, they look like they are falling out of the sky. Big ones and little ones, too.

We crouch there until almost dark, because Ring won't go home. It's like he is hypnotized. When we finally crawl away the cranes don't seem to notice; anyway, they don't fly away.

"Did you know?" Ring says. "They think they're safe here?"

"Yeah. That's what Meeker says."

"Would you like it to have to hide to be safe?"

"Jeez! I wouldn't like it."

"Neither do I." His voice is unsteady.

I look at Ring to see if he is kidding. He has a funny look on his face, but then he smiles fast and gives me a shove.

We don't talk until we are almost home. He says, "Forget what I said about hiding."

So then I can't.

Chapter 14

I like to think about the day we found the whooping cranes. I dreamed about the cranes that night after we saw them, and I think maybe Ring dreamed about them, too, because early the next morning I heard him pounding up the porch steps coming after me.

He's got a bag of sandwiches, but I make him wait while I eat my breakfast.

It doesn't take us long to get to the swamp. We practically run the whole way. It is so early in the morning everything is slippery with dew, the branches of the tree slapping us in the face like we're swimming through seaweed.

I see the cranes first. Up through the trees I

can see their white wings flashing, coming in kind of a formation like a big fan. No bouncing legs just straight like Ring when he flies—nothing to it! It makes me start laughing.

"Sh-h-h-," Ring whispers, pinching me. "See that crooked tree? That must be their landmark. They use them, you know."

They come so quickly, dipping down. I get the funny feeling they are falling out of the sky again. Ring sucks in his breath, like he didn't see them yesterday, like this is the first time.

"Meeker's right," he whispers. "They're not supposed to come this way, maybe closer to Nebraska. Meeker's not lying."

I am glad now I told Ring, and I don't care how hard Meeker thumped me on the head. "Probably a detour," I say.

They stride across in front of us like they are on parade, their skinny legs taut as rope, their heads high and proud.

Ring is counting the birds, and he holds up seven fingers. We almost don't notice two smaller ones come floating down to the crowd of whooping cranes.

"One of the big ones is missing."

"How do you know?"

"I counted, and they were in pairs yesterday. They're supposed to be."

It is real quiet. My imagination gets carried away. I think I can hear funny sounds coming from the cranes. Peeps and squeaks, what sounds like a little chitchat.

"I think those darn cranes are talking to each other. Like the little ones are crying, and the old ones are shushing them."

"Not so funny. They do. It sounds like talking." Ring must have spent all last night reading about cranes.

"Translate it for me. I wanna know what they are saying. If they are talking about me, I wanna know it."

"It ain't funny. I told you. It's sad. Only fourteen cranes left in the whole world a few years ago. People shot them when they were migrating. Just plain meanness."

Never taking his eyes off the cranes, Ring keeps dishing out bird facts, most of them revolting, things I don't want to think about. First he tells me whooping cranes can live to be thirty years old. "That's if no one shoots them." Then he asks if I ever think about being extinct. "Nobody caring if you live or die. We might all be extinct, as far as some people care."

"Oh, you're full of all sorts of cheery information today." But I had never really much thought about it—dying, I mean. I try to imagine me not being alive, being nowhere at all, zilch, nothing. It is hard to think of the world without me, and I'm not any kind of conceited monkey, either.

"It almost happened to the eagles and the falcons." Ring is talking fast, whispering, keeping his eyes on the cranes. "And it really happened to the dusky seaside sparrow, old Orange Band. He got named that, the last one living in the world, gone. They tried to save him. They even put it in the *Washington Post* when he died. Headline: Good-bye Dusky Seaside Sparrow."

"Who told you that, Fox?"

Ring didn't answer. He looked at me just blinking his eyes.

Sometimes I get mixed up. I don't know if Ring is talking about people or birds or something I don't know about. But I know a lot of times he is talking out of a book. He gets so carried away in the swamp, I get real freaky myself.

"Everyone is going to die sometime. So what? Shut up! People are going to kill birds! I don't want you telling me any more of your stories. They're downers!"

Ring is quiet for a while. We don't move around much unless the cranes move away from us, which they do, but always staying in a crowd, kind of like having their own picnic. We lay hidden in the long grass, whispering.

"You know," Ring says, "it's the sounds out here that are so scary and different. I love the sounds of things I can't see. You have to guess."

"Like what?"

"Oh, when you sense something is wrong, the way a bird or animal calls, or maybe a kid's voice changes."

"Something scary?"

"Yeah."

"I like sounds, too, like when the door is shutting at night and you're going to bed." Ring makes a terrible face at me. "I'm used to outdoor sounds, nothing to be scared of." I brag and I think what a big liar I am.

Once in a while a swarm of little birds flies low with a faint rustle of wings, and Ring rolls over on his back to watch them with his binoculars. We don't talk much at this point, not even when we eat our sandwiches.

In the middle of the afternoon there is a nervous twittering among the birds, and the whooping cranes seem to get restless. And then we hear it, a high thrusting note. And the cranes are moving, running on their long legs, taking big leaps until they are sailing in the air. Old Ring has his head tilted back, and I can tell he is flying up there with them. In a minute all that is left of them is their deep horn sounds, like a bugle. Then it is quiet.

But just then we see one whooping crane coming over the trees fast, about forty miles an hour, like someone late to church.

Ring throws his arms in the air like he's nuts. That was the missing one! I'm glad that one caught up. Ring says, "The whole darn family is heading to Wood Buffalo Park. That's where they are gonna go."

He swings his arm across my shoulders, and we walk home that way.

I wonder if I will dream about whooping cranes tonight. Suddenly I don't want to see the old swamp today. I don't want to crawl over the fence. I go home.

Chapter 15

Without thinking about it, I'm on my way to Ring's place. Josie stopped by again and left a message for me, but she spoke with Mattie, so I don't know what she said. Then Kate talked on the telephone to her, and no news.

When Josie sees me coming up the drive, she yells for me to come and sit on the fire escape with her. I wonder why she is sitting there so peaceful in the sun, drying her hair like everything is fine. She looks relaxed, her long hair blowing across her face, and she is smiling. She reaches out and takes my hand.

"How are you, Ben? I've missed you." Her voice is kind.

"Me, too."

I wait for her to tell me any news. But when she doesn't mention Ring I get scared, and I'm afraid to ask. Instead, she talks about it being so hot and dry, and she mentions that Purcell is gone for a few days. "Important business," she says before I can ask. And she nods her head and gives me that look that I think means more than her words.

Before I go she takes my hand again. "I can't tell you anything for sure. But have some faith." She gives my hand a shake. She looks at me in a way that turns me inside out. She's so calm, she makes me believe anything is possible. "Remember that, Ben."

On the way home I think about what she said, like anything really is possible with Ring. It was the same as last spring, when she took on the Spring Carnival, the biggest moneymaker of the year at Green Hills High School. At first she said, "Absolutely not!" But when they started working on it she jumped in with both feet, I think with Ring pushing her.

"With her in charge it will be different," Ring promised. Of course, he had to add, "She must have been awfully bored, or they got down on their knees to her."

Well, anyhow, it was funny how revved up Josie got. It was catching, even for Kate after a while.

At first Kate pooh-poohed it when Josie called her to give her a job, saying she didn't have time for that sort of thing. Ring got disgusted with Kate. He remarked she could stretch a little bit, let her muscles relax enough to sag.

But Kate shrugged every time Ring mentioned it to her. She said, "You know, I stay out of those sorts of things. I don't want to get involved."

Then one night we are eating supper. Ring and I had quit begging her. Kate is watching Mattie and looking out the window.

Suddenly she says, "Would it look funny if I ask my boss, old Ph.D. Delaney, for some toys to sell at the Spring Carnival? I can ask him to give me some of the seconds. Some of the ones that are splintered or rough. They toss them, you know." Kate tries to act real cool, as if it doesn't matter one way or another. "I guess I could spruce them up, good enough for her."

So after a while with no one paying much attention or begging, Kate agrees to help in a halfhearted way.

The carnival is always the first week of May

and lasts over the weekend. The whole school seems to lose its mind, especially this year with Josie leading them. She manages to hook a Ferris wheel from a nearby carnival, and also a cotton candy machine, wagon and all. I think it is because Purcell has all those connections driving a tour bus.

You don't dare get near Josie or she gives you a job. By Thursday night she has it all set up in the schoolyard, along with a hamburger stand and about a thousand colored lanterns strung from the trees, bobbing in the wind.

It had been raining, but it stops by Thursday night, and the wind is kind of soft and warm. So when we come back after supper Ring and I hook up the amplifier and start playing records over the PA system, plenty of rock and country.

The kids are coming in flocks, shuffling around, thinking they are so happy that they might explode from the excitement. Some of the cheerleaders are practicing their back-flips. It is a very happy occasion until the chief of police rides up all hot and huffy. "Don't matter if it is for the school. Keep it down!"

This kind of throws Ring. I can see he doesn't care much for cops. He turns down the music, low enough so that practically the only way you can hear it is to lay your ear against the speaker. The kids keep dancing as if they can still hear the music, but they invent their own beat and start jumping around, bopping and hopping, doing more handsprings. I remember Ring finally laughing, and he shows the kids some crazy steps they can't follow.

Then above the screaming I hear a loud screeching, and an old pickup pulls up beside us. "Do you know it is eleven o'clock?" Kate jumps out of the truck. Josie is behind the wheel with Mattie squeezed up against her.

Josie leans out of the window. "Okay, guys. We've got a job to do. Put your stuff away."

We jump in the back of the truck, and Josie drives at full speed out to a farm where she explains she has located a horse tank. It takes the four of us to load it, a tank about ten feet deep and twice the width of the truck.

The only time we'd dare drive down the road with it is at midnight, which is exactly the time the old tank starts teetering sideways. We have to drive slowly, and Mattie begins to sing in time with the jolting of the car. It is her own tune, "O, my luve's like a red, red rose."

Her words blow back to where Ring and I are packed in against the horse tank to keep it from moving, but it doesn't protect us from the midnight breeze. Ring has to button his collar. My T-shirt is billowing like a sail, with the wind going down the neck and out the bottom.

We drive back up on the school grounds near the water outlet. And while Ring and I are unloading the tank, which isn't as heavy as it looks, Josie breaks the news that it's for a dunk tank, like at the country fair. "Three balls for a dollar. Knock the kid in the water! Get it?"

She explains she's got a man to put up a home-made bull's-eye with a bell almost as big as their doorbell in case Purcell doesn't get home in time to do it.

Mattie is asleep in the cab by the time we get home, and we have to carry her into the house.

Chapter 16

The kids are overjoyed when Friday noon gets here and they are let out of school and the Spring Carnival really starts. By nighttime the colored lanterns are all lit and blowing around, and the band is playing on the school steps.

It turns out the carnival is no problem for Kate. She is selling old Ph.D. Delaney's yo-yos as fast as she can reach in the box after them. She had spent hours sanding and touching them up with paint.

She keeps Mattie by her side, grabbing her once in a while when she starts wandering off. "Here, Mattie, hold this yo-yo for me." By the end of the evening Mattie has mastered some of the art of yo-yoing. Ring showed her.

My job isn't quite as exciting. Ring elects me to be the first to get dropped in the horse tank. "What's a little water?" Ring says. "Three balls for a dollar!" he hollers. But sometimes it's not working, and I get a dunking without anyone hitting the bull's-eye and nobody paying any money.

"Bummer," Ring yells. Then I hear, "Dunk him! Dunk him!" Ring out in front is very persuasive with the ballyhoo.

Josie is keeping her eyes on everything. She floats around like a carnival spirit, her head tied up in a crazy pink turban and her big sunglasses blinking back at the lights. She is busy making little speeches through a megaphone about how the funds raised this weekend will help buy uniforms for the band. And any extra money we make? She throws her hands in the air like the sky is the limit, "Who knows." She has everyone guessing that it might be enough to add a pool to the gym or maybe have limousine service for the kids who have to walk more than a mile to school. "Anything is possible!"

I am shaking with cold. My teeth are chattering. I'm surprised there isn't ice forming on the water. Before Ring can stop me, I crawl down off the seat and out of the tank. "Your turn."

"Give me a minute." He pushes out past the crowd of people waiting, all staring at the empty seat with nobody to knock off. I smile, because it isn't gonna be me.

I watch Ring hurrying across the grounds. Josie is still talking through her megaphone. Kids are racing back and forth between the cotton candy machine and the Ferris wheel and the hamburger stand. I nearly laugh when I see some of them are ready to heave when they get off the Ferris wheel. But I don't get back up in the seat.

When Ring comes back he is eating a Baby Ruth, and he has changed into shorts and a T-shirt. He is already shivering. He crawls up on the seat and looks out over the crowd like he is sizing up the heavy hitters.

A big guy pushes up close to the tank. He keeps staring at Ring. At first Ring doesn't notice. He is shivering so hard from the cold he has to hang on to the seat to keep from falling. When they all start yelling at him, that big guy the noisiest, Ring stares up into the trees, ignoring them. Then suddenly without any warning Ring slips off the seat into the water and crawls out of the tank. He wasn't going back in, so I had to.

He doesn't say a word to me until we are

cleaning up afterward. "I suppose I looked kind of dumb falling off the seat that way."

"You didn't fall off. You did it on purpose. Why'd you do it?"

"It just hit me, why was I sitting up there waiting for some jerk to knock me in the water. Makes me feel like a big sucker!"

He counts the money and puts it in the bag. "And I don't like being stared at like I'm some kind of freak!"

"How about me? Am I a freak, or a sucker?"

"It's different with you."

"Why? Why it's different with me?"

"Oh, it doesn't matter, it's just different."

"Okay, let's forget it."

But Ring has to start in again like I'm arguing with him. "I am me." He hits his chest. "I am somebody. I don't want anybody to forget that!"

"Maybe nobody does."

Ring glares at me. "You don't know about people."

"Okay, if you say so." I'm too cold and tired to fight.

When we are ready to go home Ring is extra careful to cover the horse tank with canvas so a bird won't fall in it getting a drink or a reckless

squirrel won't drown, and I fasten it at the corners.

Before long the lights go out all over the
schoolyard. Kate brought Mattie home hours
ago. It's funny how quiet everything gets and how
people disappear like they are sucked up in a
cloud, and it seems like there are only echoes
left, caught in the trees.

I have to run hard to keep up with Ring on the
way home. He doesn't want to talk.

"Josie really jazzed up the whole place," I say.
"Best carnival we ever had. Josie scores! Really
cool! And neither one of us drowned in the tank."
I look over at him to see if he is laughing. He isn't.
"Got your Cessna? How about flying home?"

I try to imitate the way he flew in the park that
night, with my arms out, teetering a bit. He
looks at me surprised, then he puts out his arms
and smoothly begins to fly.

Chapter 17

When I wake up early this morning, the first thing I think of is Josie. She never mentioned Ring yesterday, not directly. I remember her patting my hand and smiling, saying, "Have faith." Anything is possible.

But now I have to talk about Ring. I want someone to explain what's going on. I can't go on guessing. It's making me sick.

When I go downstairs Kate has already gone to work and Mattie is yelling for me to get her breakfast. As soon as she sees me, though, the first thing she does is go out on the porch. She brings the *Gazette,* our weekly paper, to me, plopping it down on the table.

I grab it and go to my room. For about five

minutes I lay on the bed afraid to open it. When I unroll it and spread it flat on the bed, I am still afraid to look. Then I let my eyes kind of wander down over the page. It's what I didn't want to see but had to look for anyway. I get an instant belly-ache. The headline: BOY MISSING.

Now, one week later, it is all there in the paper, like it happened yesterday. One whole column about Ring, the facts about him disap-pearing and possibly drowned. His body not recovered. There are a lot of details that a news-paper feels must be mentioned. They also talk about him being a great debater and a top stu-dent. That makes me feel better.

But while I am reading my eyes start to blur so that I can't see the print. I get the shakes. I have been trying to kid myself. As though his disap-pearance isn't true, just one more of Ring's crazy stories. I crawl under my blanket and bury my head under my pillow. I stay in my room half the morning before I fold up the newspaper and take it downstairs.

After I get Mattie something to eat, I give her a stack of her magazines and I turn on the TV. Then I run most of the way out to Ring's. I really need to talk to Josie.

There is no one in the yard or on the fire

escape. Nobody yells at me when I grab the rope and ring the bell. Nobody opens the door when I pound on it. I give the rope a couple of extra jerks.

Then it hits me how quiet, how empty the house and the yard seem. No one is here; I feel sure of it. It's too quiet, the wind ruffling the leaves sounds like rain. I have a crazy thought—if I could only see through the painted windows.

I feel silly, but I can't stop looking in places where no one would hide, running all over the yard and into the little shed in back of the house where there is no sign of the pickup truck. I stay there the rest of the morning, sitting on the fire escape steps, waiting.

That night when Kate comes home she takes a quick look at me. Her face kind of puckers up. "It had to be in the paper, you know. It's news." She can't seem to keep her eyes off me, not even while she gets supper, slicing tomatoes and frying hamburgers.

Mattie puts out an extra plate for Ring. All the time we are eating she rattles on and on about him. She keeps going to the door.

"Tonight Ring is coming. I'm sure." Mattie

leans close to me and whispers, "We'll be going to New York soon."

"Oh, hell." I get up from the table, knocking my milk over.

But Kate doesn't yell at me. She comes and puts her hands on my shoulders. "Out with it."

So I unload. My worst fears. "Every time I go out, I'm looking for Ring. I never stop. I can't stop. It's like part of me knows he is gone, but another part . . . It isn't right!"

"No, it isn't."

"Sometimes I think I hear him. I dream about him."

Kate makes a little face. "Of course you do, Ben. He's your . . . "

"Nothing seems to be what you think it is, if that makes sense."

"It does, it does make sense."

I don't say anything for a moment. Then I told her, "Something else has happened."

Kate looks at me really startled now.

"When I went out to Ring's place today, there was nobody there. They're gone—Josie and Purcell. There's nobody there. I waited all morning."

That really surprises Kate. She rubs at her

nose. "She didn't say anything to me when we talked earlier. You're sure they are gone?"

"Yeah. Purcell's been gone for a few days! And something else is funny."

"What?"

"While I was waiting there on the fire escape I thought about a lot of things. Did you ever notice how different they are? I mean, Purcell and Josie from Ring. He's got light brown hair. They are really dark."

Kate laughs because she's got black hair and mine is carrot red.

"And Ring talks different, slangy. He says his words differently. And Purcell never yells at him. He soft-pedals. They all kind of soft-pedal with each other. Not like us. They're so careful."

"Acting fishy?" Kate's eyebrows go up.

"Politer."

Kate pulls herself tall and crosses her arms on her chest. "More polite?"

"Yeah, you know. And no 'Mom' or 'Pop,' either. First names."

"You call me Kate."

"Well, I'm the man of the house."

Kate stares at me amused. "How about that!

And you might say, Ring is tall and skinny like Josie."

"And I'm a runt like you."

That makes Kate laugh. "I think you're imagining things," she tells me. But she looks unsure, too.

Chapter 18

I'm not scared when I crawl over the fence into the swamp. I don't care who sees me, Meeker or anyone else. I just feel like walking around here.

I look for the grassy spot where Ring and I watched the cranes. Ring said it was their safe place. We came only once after we saw them. He wanted to be sure we wouldn't frighten them away so they'd come back in the fall.

A flock of little birds lands in the trees and bushes. If I knew much about birds, I'd guess something exciting is going on with all the wild chirping and twittering. I stand quiet and watch them for a few minutes. They are making so much noise, I have to go over and look.

When I go near the bushes where they are eating berries, some fly under and the others scatter
like spray from a fountain. I peek under the
bushes and see a few birds in the branches close
to the ground, pigging out on berries.

Out of the corner of my eye, back in the shadows, I see a pile of leaves pressed into a big
mound like a nest. I try to think what big bird
would be laying an egg here. An ostrich, maybe?
Yeah, sure. I crawl part way in to get a good look.
It is dark and silent under the bushes with the
birds gone now. I sit there staring at the nest. It is
big enough for me to curl up in. I crawl closer,
laying on my stomach, and I reach into the nest
and feel around in it. My fingers touch something, and I pull out a wad of paper. At first it
doesn't surprise me; a bird builds a nest with lots
of weird things.

I hold the paper close to my face so I can see
it, and I smell chocolate. I press it open and stare
at a crushed Baby Ruth wrapper in my hand. I
begin to shake and I drop the wrapper and get
out of there fast.

I feel so cold, like I touched a ghost, I go sit in
the sun. What's the matter with me? A lot of kids
eat Baby Ruths. But it makes my hair stand on

end. And then for a minute I hold my breath. I'm sure I hear him laughing. I run down into the wet grass, past the dead trees. I keep listening for him, but all I hear now are some old trees branches rubbing together.

And now I can't stop the tears running down my cheeks and I bury my face in the grass. I feel like I'm bruised all over. The candy wrapper is a sign, I'm sure. Then I think I hear a voice, somebody talking to me.

"Don't go to pieces. Make yourself do what you expect you can do. That's control. Get it?" That was Ring's favorite pep talk to himself, and to me.

So I shut my eyes and I sit for a long time listening, but I know there is no one here but me. I go back to the nest and push things around, but there's nothing else. I put the Baby Ruth wrapper back exactly where I found it, and I head home.

Mattie is taking a nap when I get there. I'm glad because she asks so many snoopy questions. But when she gets up she doesn't even look at me; instead she goes to the window and looks up and down the street, as usual. "Has the mailman come?" she asks.

I sit on the porch steps with Mattie waiting for the mailman to bring her a million dollars. That makes her happy, especially when she thinks I am waiting for a million dollars, too. She talks about Ring like she's forgotten that he is gone.

"I will be going to New York to see the Statue of Liberty," she tells me. "Ring will drive me."

"Okay. Okay! That's nice."

I try to relax and breathe easy. I let my mind go galloping. Mattie keeps talking. She sounds like a little lost bird, repeating, repeating.

When Kate gets home she gives me the once over, as usual trying to read my mind. She walks over to me real close. "What's happened now?"

"Nothing's happened." I turn away when she tries to look into my eyes.

She shakes her head and pats me on the back and leaves her hand there for a minute.

I pretend to eat supper, and the food gags me. I watch TV and go to bed early. I can hear Mattie thumping through her magazines in bed and laughing at the pictures.

But I'm so nervous I can't sleep. All I can think about is that Baby Ruth candy wrapper. Every time I close my eyes, that is all I see. A lot of stuff starts going around in my head. For one thing, you can't eat a Baby Ruth if you're dead, and no one has any proof that Ring drowned. That Baby Ruth candy wrapper is a sign. Anyway, I know there is something I have to do tonight.

I lay there in bed a long time until Mattie quits laughing and settles down and Kate is breathing heavy. Then I jump out of bed and jerk on my jeans and get out the back door fast. I'd get banged on the head if Kate caught me.

And I run, run out to the swamp. It sure is different at night—no sun, no squawking birds. It is so totally black and quiet, I feel scared stiff and lonelier than I've ever felt before, like I might be the last person on earth. And I think of Ring, and I wonder if he is lonely, if he is somewhere in the dark, too. And I starting listening for him again.

I push my way through the brush, and I scramble from tree to tree. I can smell dead leaves and decayed wood. Whenever something touches my face I pray it is only a moth. I try not to imagine the size of any spiders hanging over me in the branches, waiting to smother me in their webs.

A sound gradually comes to me, a constant buzzing. It is probably ten million mosquitoes and lightning bugs all jammed together making this peculiar noise that is really getting on my nerves.

And then the wings start, a quiet fanning of the air, and all I can think of is bats. For away, up in the park, I hear an old screech owl. It sounds as if someone is wringing its neck.

It's harder to find the place under the bushes in the dark. I have to feel my way along the ground, scared I might touch a body, maybe a snake or a rat. But all I touch are leaves, cold and slimy. I feel all around in the nest until I find the candy wrapper. Then I keep feeling around and around. But there's nothing new there. I go kind of limp for a minute. I don't know what I expected, maybe to touch Ring.

But still, at least there's the wrapper. It is like touching something alive, talking to me. Because I am sure now it is a message from Ring. A sign he was here. He was here. He was here!

It scares the heck out of me. It makes me sick, and I can't let him down. And it makes me feel bad to think he's hiding somewhere and I don't know how to help him.

I reach into the leaves again and pick up the wrapper and shove it into my pocket, and then I run like the devil is after me. When I get home I hide the wrapper under my mattress and crawl into bed.

When my heart quits pounding so hard I try to talk to God. I don't pray very often, but tonight I don't have anyone else I dare talk to.

"God, please take care of Ring, wherever he is. Whatever he is doing, please help him. And please let me know what to do. I'd just like to know before Ring gets into more trouble. And please let him be safe." As an afterthought I whisper, "And mum's the word about the candy wrapper."

The window is wide open and so full of light it keeps me awake. And I am hoping maybe in the night Ring might try to crawl through it. He did that sometimes just to surprise me. I watch until I fall asleep.

Chapter 19

Josie and Purcell are still gone. So the first thing in the morning we are on our way down to see Meeker. Kate's got me by the elbow and insists. She says there's no need to go to the police yet and get somebody arrested or mixed up in something. But since Meeker's a conservation officer, in Kate's mind he's next best, and he's also a friend.

"We've got to report Ring's folks are gone, if they don't already know it. That's what my boss, old Ph.D. Delaney says."

But when we tell Meeker he doesn't act too surprised. All he says is, "They must have a good reason. The strain must be unbearable." He pats me on the shoulder.

I guess that's exactly what melts me down. I look Meeker in the eyes and confess that Ring and I had gone over the fence into the swamp and that we had seen the cranes. But I sure don't mention going out yesterday and finding the Baby Ruth candy wrapper. I think I'm kind of protecting Ring, and me, too.

Well, he's really surprised. Meeker acts peeved at first, but then his face warms up, kind of soft with some pity mixed in.

He pats me on the shoulder again instead of thumping me, as he'd threatened to do if I ever breathed a word about the cranes. Any fool can see he thinks he is talking to a very upset boy, and he isn't going to make it any worse for me. And I feel a lot better for mentioning the cranes.

So it's Meeker who breaks the story in Green Hills about Ring's folks being gone and also the possibility that maybe Ring didn't drown, his own hunch.

Later on, after our meeting with him, Meeker makes a trip out to the toy factory to see Kate, which I discover as soon as she walks in the door tonight, for she immediately turns on the TV and says, "Meeker says to watch the news tonight."

We get in on the tail end of a story about some

kid several people reported seeing hitchhiking down Highway 30. They said that when they offered him a ride he refused. He didn't talk. He just shook his head. They thought maybe he was deaf and dumb. Before the officers could pick him up he was gone, disappeared like he left on a cloud. No one could describe him, every story was different.

Kate takes a deep breath and shakes her head. "Well, it can't be Ring. You can't shut him up."

"He can talk a mile a minute," I agree. But I want to hear more about the kid. I want to know if he was eating a Baby Ruth. I want to tell Kate that Ring left me a sign, but I can't.

I hear the TV the next morning before I get out to bed. Mattie's playing with it. I hear a dozen stations before she stops. My ears prick up when I hear the news and a voice droning on and on about the mystery boy, the same as last night.

The voice says they are checking for missing kids across the country. He gives an 800 number and says, "Please call if you are missing. At least go for help. Call home!" When he says, "Rain tomorrow." I run downstairs and turn the TV off.

Meeker comes over in the evening and asks us

what we thought about the news report. He shrugs when we both shake our heads. He says, "Just an off chance."

"Ring's not deaf and dumb," I say.

"You can't shut him up," Kate says. "Not if he wants to talk."

"And he wouldn't be hitchhiking down 30," I add. "That's not his style. He might be *running* down 30 . . . "

Meeker put his hat on. "Just an idea."

But Meeker's easygoing attitude is good for me. It's like he is telling me to cool it. It doesn't help to get excited, because we can't change anything . . . we can only wait.

I want to be calm like Meeker and not go to pieces over the candy wrapper. Meeker isn't one to run his mouth anyway, except for the time he told me about the whooping cranes, and he is probably sorry for that. But I still can't tell him about the Baby Ruth.

By the next morning I am on my way back to the swamp. I've just got to look again. The little birds are still hanging in there eating berries. When I look under the bushes I can see where they have been scratching and digging in the dirt. The leaves under the bushes don't look any different, except where the birds have been poking. It's still a big nest, and there's nothing new in it.

And there is nobody waiting for me, nobody hiding here. I make sure by walking and wading from one end of the swamp to the other. The wind is blowing and I can smell the swamp, and everything seems so ordinary and ugly. Nothing's changed. Ring hasn't been back.

By the afternoon the easygoing Meeker attitude has worn off, through, and I feel like I might fall on my face. The reason is the five o'clock news.

When I turn on the TV I hear the guy talking about the mystery boy again, like his real name is "Mystery Boy." He tells how the kid was described by a man who saw him hitchhiking: "Tall, and hard to tell his age, and skinny. He was wearing a cap with a big bill."

It's a small thing, but no, Ring wouldn't be caught dead in a cap. Not even when it rains. No, it's not Ring.

That night the two policemen come out to talk to me. They ask me a million questions, starting with a dumb one. "Were Ring and you friends?" They already know the answer, or they wouldn't be out here.

Kate sits across from me giving me eye signals, like she is trying to feed the answers to me.

Then they start asking questions that really make me mad. "Did Ring have a reason to run away? Did he have any problems? Would he try to hurt himself? Would he try to drown himself?"

I am so squeezed up on the inside, I almost choke yelling, "No!"

Then the cop with the beefy nose asks if I know who that kid is, the one seen hitchhiking down Highway 30.

"I don't know."

Just when they are ready to leave Mattie comes in. She is happy to see them and she shakes their hands. At first I am sure she thinks they are delivering her million dollars.

She goes to the door and looks down the street, and over her shoulder she says, "Ring will be here any minute."

That kind of starts things again. The policemen look at each other, and then back at me. The fat one sits back down, kicking over a geranium, and the other one goes out on the porch to smoke. Kate doesn't say a thing. In a few minutes Mattie talks about the postman bringing her a million dollars. She explains to them that Ring is

going to take her to look for a Ford in the morning. And suddenly they can't get out of there fast
enough.

But I get to thinking about everything they
asked me and about how many times I lied or
twisted things around and not telling all I knew.
And any lies I might have told them are curled up
inside me, giving me cramps. I think I'm getting
diarrhea.

Chapter 20

The next morning the guy on TV gets off Ring's back, just a word or so about him still missing, nothing new. I am glad. Every time I see old perfect teeth smiling and talking about missing kids, it is like an electrical shock running through me.

Kate tells me to settle down, relax. She says it doesn't do any good worrying, wearing myself to a frazzle. So I try tuning everything out, but I can't.

But then in the afternoon Mattie has the TV blaring. I can't help but hear it. "There are strange new facts coming to light." The crazy TV is screaming the words. I turn it off.

I want to hear it, and I don't want to hear it. I

take off out the door, so I *can't* hear it. I go for a long walk along the river, then I run until I'm tired and I sit on the bank and watch how fast the water is flowing today.

And I can see Ring, his face bobbing in the water, laughing, his arms like oars pushing him along. I start talking to him. "Why do you do these things?" I start yelling. "Why can't it be hunky-dory like it used to be? Kate says it's making me skinny. Don't you care?"

When I get home Mattie is waiting on the porch, not for me, but for the mailman. I almost choke trying to hold back a horrible snicker, like I might be having hysterics. It relieves me, though. At least one thing never changes.

Mattie is always waiting. She waits and waits, the same as me, only it doesn't bother her because every morning she gets up and starts waiting again. She's sure her millions will come. But will Ring?

She follows at my heels into the house, chattering like a little squirrel. And for a while I try to shut out everything and listen to Mattie.

By five o'clock I can't resist anymore. I have to turn on the news. What I have been waiting for comes along at the end. "The mystery boy has been identified. The young hitchhiker was located on a bus traveling in Ohio."

I close my eyes and take a big breath.

"The boy has been missing for almost a year from a boys' home in Winfield, Ohio." The voice is droning on and on. I want to bat it away. I've heard enough.

That can't be Ring. Not in a Home for Boys. He's got Josie and Purcell.

The news anchor keeps talking. "He is a ward of the state of Ohio. No living relatives."

Ring was always talking about his family. I know it can't be Ring.

Then I hear the boy's name, as loud and clear as if it were written across the sky in bright lights, making booms and blinking like Fourth of July fireworks. Up there where everybody can see. Flashing off and on: "Fox."

Fox! Fox! Fox!

I take a deep breath. I feel like someone has knocked me sideways. I go over and turn off the TV. It's not adding up for me. It doesn't make sense.

Mattie comes and stands in front of me. "Don't cry, Ben. You'll shrink up to nothing."

"Hell, I'm not crying." I rub my cheek hard.

She slaps me on my butt, then lightly on my face. I feel her skinny little arms go tight around my waist and her head on my chest. Then she starts singing her crazy little song.

I yell, "Stop it!" But I let Mattie hold my hand, and I let her pull me to the window to look for the postman.

Chapter 21

Kate must have heard the news at work, for she comes rushing up the walk and in the door.

"Ben! What do you make of it? What are they saying on TV?"

"I don't know. I . . . "

Kate takes me by the shoulders. She makes me look her straight in the eyes. "Ring has a friend named Fox, doesn't he?"

I nod, feeling miserable.

"Well, it can't be Ring then, and they don't mention two kids. Too bad." And I see her lips are quivering.

"Maybe they were going to meet somewhere."

"That would be good, wouldn't it? He might help find Ring." Kate nods her head.

I go up to my room so I don't have to listen to Kate. I think of all the stories that Ring told me about Fox. All the kooky things that Fox did. We laughed about Fox. And I was jealous of Fox. That's a real hoot, but I guess I had reason.

For a minute I think I'm going to laugh and cry all at once, kind of like I'm nuts. The trouble is, how do I separate Fox and Ring? I wonder who came to the swamp and left the candy wrapper, Fox or Ring? Were they playing tricks on me?

I am suddenly so tired, I lay down on my bed. I close my eyes. I think I hear Ring's voice, just as plain. "Ben, I think I'm going to learn to fly."

And I see him put his arms out like wings on a plane and then tilt them just so, and he runs without any kind of bouncing. I can hear him laughing like a plane going away, getting fainter and fainter until I can't hear it anymore. I must have been dreaming, but the dream stays in my mind in a warm sort of way, and I sleep all night.

The next morning Mattie is slapping me awake like she thinks I'm dead. The sun has been shining on me, and I am all sweaty.

"Come down and eat your breakfast."

I won't let Mattie turn on the TV all day. I mow the grass without her nagging me, and she follows me most of the time.

I am waiting for Kate to get home. I can take it better when she tells me something new herself. It is easier for me to believe.

She starts in with a pep talk. "Some things we can't control. Remember."

"Yeah."

While we are eating supper Kate insists we listen to the news. "Good or bad!"

"I guess."

"We've got to face it—whatever."

"Okay."

The guy on TV is giving the weather in a very detailed way. Then I hear the name Fox. And naturally I quit eating. The guy slides into a story about the unusual facts surrounding Fox, the boy who wouldn't talk—"Didn't open his mouth," is the way he puts it.

But the point the news guy is making is what caused Fox to start talking. At first I don't get it. Then I don't believe what I'm hearing. The guy is describing a bird, a small bluebird they found in the boy's pocket.

"It looks like a Christmas tree ornament," the guys says. "It's missing a few feathers and has a bell fastened to its neck." Then he repeats what Fox said: "Don't touch that! Leave it alone. It's valuable." He makes the kid sound awfully silly.

Kate is watching me. She tells me to start eating my food before it gets cold.

And then it hits me. The bird. I saw it in his room. Perched on Ring's headboard, a funny little bluebird with a few feathers missing and a bell around its neck.

Ring had yelled and grabbed it away from me when I touched it. "I don't want you touching that! I've had it a long time." That's exactly what he said. And he put it away in a drawer.

I jump up from the table and go out and sit on the porch steps. Kate comes out and she looks at me, then she leaves me alone. I lean my head on my knees: I wouldn't want anyone to see my face.

I sit there for a long time. I have to think. The bird. It belongs to Ring, not Fox. Josie and Purcell would know that, too. The stories, all the stories that Ring told me about Fox: sleeping in a tree, the fruit freak, sleeping in the rain, hiding in a store all night. Iffy things. And if they did happen, it wasn't to a kid named Fox. All those things happened to Ring. He was safe! They found him. I feel like I'm burning up. Maybe all along Ring was really trying to tell me the truth? I would like to believe that. And then I start to cry. He was trying to tell me, and I never understood.

And then I stop crying and start thinking. I can't figure out why he'd run away like a scared rat and worry us sick. That I don't understand. I hit the step with my fist so hard it hurts. Then I take off down the road so I don't have to talk to anyone.

When I get home I rush upstairs to bed but Kate runs into my room after me.

"Ring! They've found Ring. That boy, he *was* Ring. It wasn't Fox. Purcell found him on the bus."

"I know."

"You know? You *know?* Why didn't you tell me?"

I'm quiet for a long time. But Kate just stands there and waits for me. "I was trying to figure it out, it didn't make sense." Then I shout at her, "He scared the hell out of us! And why did he call himself Fox?"

Kate comes over and gives me a shake, then she hugs me. "Ben, Ben, he's safe! That's what matters!"

I don't know what to say. I'm suddenly so angry, and I need Kate to leave. But Kate babbles on.

"Josie called. She sounded so happy!" Kate sits on the foot of my bed. "Ben, he's found. It's okay. You can let it go now. He's okay. Things happen that we don't understand. Some day we will."

I was quiet for a moment. "Do you think he'll tell me what happened?"

Instead of answering, Kate asks me another question. "Did you know about the bird? The bird he brought with him?"

"That's when I knew for sure that kid had to be Ring," I told her. "I saw the bird once. He wouldn't let *me* touch it, either. I thought it was funny."

"He must have a very good reason." Kate kisses me on the cheek before she leaves. "He's your friend. Maybe he will tell us when we see him."

Later, when I hear her getting ready for bed and Mattie still turning pages in her magazine and talking to herself, I think about Ring coming home, where it's safe. I leave my window open anyway.

Chapter 22

So now I'm waiting again. Waiting for Ring to come home.

The police don't come out to see me anymore. From now on, it's Ohio's problem, they say. And Kate worries out loud about what the gossip around town might be. I know it is Josie and Purcell she is thinking about. "It's so strange," she says. "Didn't you ever get a hint from Ring that they weren't—"

"But they are!" I shake my head. I think of his room with the painted window, the lighthouse and the sea, and all his bird books. "They treat him good. They *are* family."

"But they're not really *his* family, his parents."

When Kate says that, it scares me. Maybe he won't be coming back.

And that's what worries both of us. "We'll be getting the answers soon," Kate says. "Josie promised when she called. She is with him now." She looks at me, her eyes bright. "You're right—he does have a family."

Meeker comes to see us. And to cheer me up, he reminds me of the whooping cranes. "Come October," he says, and he gives me a nod. I get the feeling he'd look the other way if I went over the fence into the swamp again to find the cranes.

For a few days Mattie doesn't stop staring at the TV. She sits, her knees almost touching it, expecting to see Ring suddenly appear, like he's going to jump out of the set. But when he doesn't she goes back to watching for the mailman again. And life starts to get more normal.

I keep the grass mowed so short, a sheep couldn't survive. Kate says it is good to keep busy and try not to think too much. I'm getting so my mind doesn't open and close with Ring, and I try to think of trivial things, like who might win the World Series.

But I still look for him everywhere I go.

Mattie is the one who brings me the letter with my name written on it. And then she hangs on to it, and I have to take it away from her.

I read it out loud to her:

Dear Ben,

We are sorry for what happened. We miss
you terribly. I don't know how soon we will
be returning. Not too long. There are things
to untangle, get sorted out. One day we will
be able to sit down with you and explain.

From all of us,

Our love,

Josie

There is no mention of Ring—or Fox. But she
includes him in the "we" and "us" parts. Kate says
to get busy and answer. She practically dictates
my whole letter, short as it is:

Dear Josie and All,

Glad to get your letter. We miss you, too.
When are you coming home? Mattie says
hello, and she is looking forward to her
trip to New York. Be sure and tell Ring.

Kate sends her regards.

See you soon,

Ben

Time really gets boring after the letter from
Josie because I start waiting for another letter the
very next day.

If it weren't for Meeker being extra cheerful and bringing us ice cream every couple of days, it would have been a dull week. Every once in a while Meeker and I walk over to school to look at the new addition.

And then we get another letter from Winfield, Ohio.

Dear Ben and Mattie and Kate,
Thinking of you. I am sorry things are going so slowly, but I think it is working out. Purcell is on the road most of the time. So it is up to me. I worry about our place. Ben, if you will check on it once in a while, I would appreciate it very much. We left in such a hurry, I didn't get to talk to you. It is good to hear from you.

> All our love,
> Josie

There is another folded paper in the envelope. A note, very short.

Hey Ben,
I am alive. Don't worry.

> Keep your nose clean,
> Ring

I start going out to their place every day to check on it, which I had been doing, but now it is different. I'm so uptight, antsy. Sometimes I ring the bell, sometimes ten times just for the heck of it. The sound makes me feel kind of wild and reckless. Then I go to the top step of the fire escape and I look down the road.

And I wonder what it'll be like to see Ring again. I don't even know how to act around him, because I don't know what's going on. I don't know anything for sure.

So I write to Josie and tell her how things are, that the grass is getting brown and that the weeds along the drive are as tall as trees. And I always start off with, "Hello everybody," meaning Ring. But at the end of the letter I write, "P.S. Hello you old sucker. Shape up or ship out!" Meaning, Ring, come home.

Then I get a letter from Josie saying they will be home soon. As crazy as it sounds, I get sick to my stomach. I can't eat my supper. All I wanted was for Ring to come back and now I don't know what to do—I feel scared almost.

Chapter 23

My routine has become set: in the mornings I go out and check the place for Josie, and before I go home I always crawl to the top of the fire escape and look down the road. At night I sit on our porch steps looking up the street. Sometimes Kate sits with me. She brings me a glass of lemonade. I can tell she doesn't want me waiting like this. But she never says a thing.

It has been three days since Josie's last letter. It is the second week of August. Ring has been gone since the last week of June. I am getting so tired of waiting, and it is raining tonight so I come in the house. Mattie is looking out the window, eating a peanut butter sandwich. "The mailman won't come until morning," I tell her.

I go up to bed and I'm just about undressed when Kate yells to me, "I hear someone at the door. Can you let them in?"

My legs don't want to hold me up. It's sinking in, who the person on the porch might be. I zip up my pants on the way downstairs. When I open the door I hang on to it for a minute. I see someone move back toward the steps, as if they are uncertain, too. My eyes smart like heck. When Kate turns on the porch light, I can see a shadow on the steps. Then he comes closer, a big kid, his hair short, buzzed. He seems even taller. He is thinner, too, which makes his face look all squeezed up. His mouth is clamped shut, but I can see his chin quivering. I never ever saw him cry. And I hold my breath, so I won't do anything silly.

But Mattie lets out a scream and ducks around me and puts her skinny little arms around his waist and lays her head on his chest. "Ring!"

It gives me time to get a hold of myself and get used to the idea that this is Ring—or Fox. I keep looking to see if he seems different in any other ways. I almost expect him to be. We stare at each other until it is almost funny, like we never saw each other before. But when he tries to smile and clamps his big hand on my shoulder and squeezes, I know he isn't that much different. At least not that I can notice. Kate hugs him then and really hangs on.

But just when things seem to be settling down, I suddenly feel unhinged.

I jerk away from him, and I feel my nerves go in one big splash. I get the shakes and start laughing all at the same time. I am glad to see that Ring is shaken up too. I can see it in his eyes. Then he squeezes them shut, and a tear leaks out.

We don't look at each other much after that. He talks to Mattie, and she hangs on to him while he explains he didn't forget about the trip or about her or any of us. He talks mostly to her. I think it is easier for him, but I know he is talking to me, too.

After a while I can see he is getting restless, and he jumps up and grabs my arm. "Want to run around the block?" He gives my arm a tug. "I need to."

So it's Ring and me, or maybe Fox and me, walking, then running side by side, like we always have. It has quit raining, just a mist that feels cool on my face. I think he wants to talk to me, but he doesn't say a word. All I hear are his old sneakers slapping the pavement like a wet towel, and I can hear his tuneless whistle, but it is real, not something driving me nuts.

I watch his face. I can't read a thing. I want to

scream. I want to yell at him. I want to ask him a million questions. I want to say, "Open up, or I'll slug you!" I don't. Once he stops and looks at me, and I think he is going to tell me something. But he just stares at me for a minute. I keep quiet. He looks too beat and bruised, like he got sucked up in a tornado.

I run halfway out to his house with him before I turn around to come home. I'm going around the corner when I hear him yelling, "Ben!" When I turn around he's waving his arms like he always did.

"Call me Ring. It's okay. I want you to. The same old Ring. Remember, don't ever call me Fox!" He starts running again, but he turns around once more. "Sorry for everything."

It starts raining again before I get home. I hope Ring makes it without getting wet. I should have gone the whole way with him tonight.

Chapter 24

I don't see much of Ring at first. When he does come over he isn't very talkative. He spends most of his time listening to Mattie, who clings to him.

A couple of times I walk out to his place to see if we can talk. When we are alone Ring and I are both edgy. And he sits there like a dummy. You wouldn't think he is the fastest talker in town. Sometimes I try to stare him down. He doesn't guess that part of me would like to kick him in the middle, punch him out, and just to hear him yell "ouch!"

So Ring still hasn't explained why he ran away. Kate says be patient. It will all come out in the wash. There are some things that have to be settled yet. And even though I have the urge to pop him one, I'm worried stiff about why he was in that boys' home and if he might have to go back.

Then early one morning Ring pounds on the door and yells, "Let's go!" Like nothing's changed, everything's just hunky-dory. He doesn't give me a chance to finish my breakfast, just like old times. He's got his binoculars hanging around his neck, and he is eating a ham sandwich.

It's a stormy kind of day, and the sun is zigzagging through the clouds, making it cool in the shade. At one point when the sun is shining on his face and he is smiling at me, it hits a nerve, and I can see him that day at the picnic when he disappeared under a wave. I clench my hands and start breathing so hard that it sounds like I'm crying.

I run on ahead of him, and we crawl over the fence and walk down the path to the swamp. Without a word, we sit on the little hump of grass not far from the bushes where we watched the cranes.

"I wonder if they will come back," he says finally.

"The whooping cranes?"

He nods.

"In about six weeks."

I watch to see if he looks over to the bushes where he left the Baby Ruth candy wrapper. But Ring points his binoculars toward the sky at a bunch of swallows. I lay staring at the sky, silently, too. I watch the clouds flowing fast across, and I wait.

I am almost asleep when I hear Ring talking. His voice is low, hard to hear. It's funny, when Ring starts telling me what I want to hear it comes slowly, like a trickle of water. Never straight out, but in bits and pieces, like all of his stories about Fox.

"It was a rotten thing to do. I really didn't plan it that way. It just kind of hit me. At first it was sort of a game when I walked into the river."

"A game! Gawd!" I sit up so I can look at him.

He keeps on talking, faster now. "I know, crazy. I couldn't have drowned in that river unless I had a heart attack or someone tied a rock around my neck. Who would think I drowned?"

"All of us! We all thought you drowned!" I shout.

"Yeah. I found out later."

"The fire department brought a boat!"

"Skip it."

"They kept going up and down the river. They dragged the river for three days!"

"Skip it!" Ring glares at me.

"You scared us out of our minds!" I was standing now. He turns his head away from me.

When he looks at me again his face has softened. "See, at first I was just treading water, then I let myself go under and I swam underwater. It was easier to keep going. I know it sounds really crazy."

"Yeah, it does sound really crazy."

"And when I stopped at the swamp, it still was like playing a game, but I was getting a little scared. I gave you a chance to find me. I thought you'd think of the swamp and guess that I might stop there. I waited for you. I *waited* for you, Ben. And I thought how we could surprise everybody."

"You didn't wait long enough. I did come. I found your nest." He is deadpan when I look at him.

He takes a deep breath, and it comes out in a soft laugh. "My nest."

"And I read your message. The Baby Ruth candy wrapper."

"You did find it! You came!" His eyes glistened. "I was trying to tell you the truth, so you'd know."

"I know. And I had to lie about it. I was afraid to tell anyone. I wanted you to come back. More than anything, I wanted you to be safe. Why would you do that to me? I thought you were my friend." I turn to look at him. "I hid the darn candy wrapper. Even when the police came."

Ring sits quiet. It isn't until he spots a red-winged blackbird and stares through his binoculars as the bird flies away that he starts talking again.

"I stayed here half the night before I left. I had time to think of all kinds of things happening that scare me. Mostly about Josie and Purcell. I didn't mean to hurt them. For a long time I was having bad dreams—nightmares. I'd see them behind bars, in jail, and it was all because of me." He nods his head. I don't really understand, but I know I need to keep quiet. Let him go on.

He's quiet for a long time, and every once in a while I see him looking at me like he's trying to read my mind. "It was nothing, for me, running away. I've done it a lot of times. I just stay on country roads and hide when I hear a car."

It gives me goose bumps just to hear him talk that way. "But it's crazy and it's mean! Why would you do that? For a joke? A *joke?*"

Ring goes on talking like he doesn't hear me. "There was an old man who was backing his car out of his driveway and told me to jump in. He gave me a ride most of the way to Mississippi. He kept talking about his dead wife and how he was waiting to follow her. I felt sorry for him because he had no family left."

"Too bad you couldn't feel sorry for us."

Ring ignored me. "He let me out at a store at the edge of a little town. He put a ten-dollar bill in my pocket. A couple of cars tried to pick me up, but I played dumb."

Then Ring talks about a park on the Mississippi River where he stayed and slept in a pavilion. He had one hamburger a day, and fruit doesn't cost much, he says.

I interrupt him. "Especially if you steal it. Okay, so you're the old fruit freak!" And for the first time that day I feel like laughing, and Ring does, too, like we're coming unwound.

"Heck, if it's half rotten or bruised, take it out of the bin so no one gets cheated." And before I can ask him how he managed to get away with that, he says, "And I suppose you want to know all my other stories, about me breaking into the zoo? I guess you could call it breaking back in. Every time they caught me running away, they marched me right back to the Home for Boys, the zoo. Every time I ran away."

"The zoo, that's what you call it?"

"Yeah." Ring gets serious again. He talks about riding a bus for a couple of days using the last money he had. "Nobody asked me questions. Nobody noticed me much."

"Well, hey. You made everyone believe you were dumb. Probably not a hard job."

He takes a deep breath, and it comes out in another soft laugh. "I know."

Ring goes on talking like he can't stop now. All about how he was curled up on the seat in the bus and someone tapped his shoulder. It was Purcell bending over him. "He didn't grab me, but I knew he wanted to. When I wasn't found the first few days, Josie and Purcell suspected I might be headed this way toward Ohio, back where I came from. Bus drivers kind of keep tabs on things for each other. Messages go across the country like sending a letter. That's the way Purcell tracked me down."

"I'd have killed you if I were Purcell!"

"He had a right to. They knew I had run away a lot of times. It wasn't such a shock."

Ring jumps up and walks over to the bushes and looks under. "Just like I left it. Thank you."

I just look at him, then I ask, "I suppose you slept in your nest!"

He shakes his head. "What would you say if I told you I was running away when I came here with Josie and Purcell?"

"I'd say you were a liar."

"I ran away from the Home and followed them."

"Then you must have flipped your lid to run away again."

"Okay, maybe I did flip my lid—but it's the truth."

"I don't get you." And I wasn't trying to give him a hard time; I really didn't understand.

"Maybe you don't. I lived with them in Ohio a whole year. They didn't have kids—only me. See, they thought we were just going to pack up and all of us leave together, move to another state when Purcell got the new job. It didn't happen. It was hell for them to have to tell me. Josie said they'd be back as soon as they could work through the legal mess. She cried when she told me, 'We didn't dream you couldn't go with us,' she'd said." Ring made a terrible face. "You know me. I couldn't wait. I was a foster kid they were taking care of. We don't have many rights. I had to follow them!"

We sit quiet a few minutes. Me, I'm trying to

soak up all he's telling me. I feel kind of mean and ashamed. Ring's quiet, like he's through explaining. I don't know what to say. Then I can see him making up his mind.

"I was a foster kid my whole damn life," he says. His eyes are kind of squinty when he looks at me. "It's no big deal. Plenty of kids to go around in this world. I've been in a pile of foster homes." He stops and looks at me for a minute to see how I'm taking it. "The only place I ever wanted to stay was with Josie and Purcell. That was the only place in all my life."

"Yeah, I could see how you'd want to stay with them."

"They were working on adopting me. Only in Ohio—well, the Social Services Department said I still belonged to them. That I couldn't go to another state. All that bull and a lot of legal garbage about who has custody."

Ring's concentrating, his eyes staring straight ahead, and he has to blink. When he starts talking again, it's slowly. I can see it is hard for him. "I stayed with them until the night before they left. I helped them pack the trailer they were pulling. They brought me home as late as they dared. I watched out the dorm window when they drove away. They honked their horn and blinked their lights. I waved and waved, I just kept waving . . . until all I could see was my hand in the window waving back at me." He takes a deep breath, but when I look at him I'm surprised—he is grinning. "I disappeared that night, too. See, I said that's the easiest thing in the world for me to do, run away."

"Well, maybe. I never tried it." Ring's quick change of mood has made me feel a little better.

Ring rolls over on his stomach, his chin propped in his hands. He keeps looking at me, then he asks, "Do you know how to pick a lock?"

"I'm taking lessons right now." I try to be funny.

"I'll show you sometime. It's easy."

He's quiet for a while. In a little bit he starts talking about sneaking out of the dorm that night and going back to Josie and Purcell's place and hiding in their trailer. It wasn't hard to get in. "I slept rolled up in the bedding under the seat. I woke up when I heard the car starting and felt the trailer moving. It was still dark outside. Josie didn't bother to look in the trailer all that first day."

"You sure lucked out."

But when they stopped for hamburgers, Ring says he about passed out from the smell of food. He grins at me again. "I was lucky. There was a toilet and water and stuff in the cupboard, bread and peanut butter and some apples. So I didn't starve. The worst part was it was so darn hot I took off most of my clothes."

I am so glad to finally be able to laugh. I can see Ring sitting in the trailer naked, the sweat running down his legs, and a policeman stopping them. I keep giggling.

But Ring is talking again. "I was glad they stayed in a motel the first night. It gave me a chance to open the windows and cool down. It was the next night they found me when they pulled into a campground." He rolls his eyes.

Ring has a hard time when he tries to describe the terrible shock it was to Josie and Purcell when they saw him. "They went bananas. Josie started crying and hugging me. She was glad to see me, but she was scared as hell. See, she just couldn't stop crying. 'We were coming back!' she kept saying to me."

Ring's face tightens up, looking scared. "And Purcell clamped on to my arm so hard I thought he was going to break it. 'Why?' he asked me.

'Do you know they can pick us up and arrest the whole bunch of us? Child stealing! Kidnapping! You have to go back!'"

Ring is giving me goose bumps. He tries to hurry over the part about begging to go with them. "It was a horrible scene. I keep yelling, 'Don't take me back! Let me go with you. I'll just run away again. I'll keep running. You will never find me again.'" Ring glares at me. "I really meant that!"

Then he calms down a bit and goes, "And Purcell walked around the trailer, kicking up a lot of dirt, almost making a rut. He said the words over and over, 'Why wouldn't you wait?' Sometimes he'd look at me, and I'd shake my head and yell, 'I won't go back!' I should have been kicked in the butt." Ring rolls over on his back and looks at me.

I'm really upset by all he's telling me. I sit up and pretend I'm looking at a bird in the top of the dead tree, and I keep staring until my eyes water.

Ring is quiet for a minute, too. Then he starts again. "When we got so tired that none of us could make sense, Purcell said, 'We'll sleep on it.'" And Ring tells me about Josie going across the street to get a bag of hamburgers and a bottle of milk. "They insisted that I eat most of the hamburgers."

"Well, that wasn't too hard, was it?"

Ring looks at me and sighs. He doesn't think it's funny. "We started driving early the next morning, me squeezed in between them. They didn't say word. They just kept driving."

Chapter 25

Ring and I watch the birds for a while. There is a cloud of them over us. We sit about half an hour more. I think that must be all that Ring's going to tell me. Maybe I'll never hear the end of his story. Then he starts talking again.

It seems easier for him now, and he smiles when he says, "We never did turn back. We just kept driving straight ahead." And he tells me about camping every night for the next few months. About how every time they came to a nice park by a lake, they would stay for a while. He tries to describe to me how he felt seeing the sun come up over the lake, all the funny shadows it made, and walking into the trees where it was cool green and pine trees smelled like mint. "It was like a regular vacation. The kind I never ever went on before. Purcell painted a few portraits for fifteen dollars a piece and lots of woodsy scenes for campers which he sold for only five bucks a picture."

Ring's voice is softer now, and he sounds happy. "Purcell had to forget the job he was planning on, and he didn't start looking for another one until we were through Illinois. But after stopping at only a couple of places, he got one driving a tour bus. The company's headquarters were on the Iowa-Minnesota border. So we headed in that direction."

"Hey, it's not a bad job. Driving a bus all over the country."

Ring looks a me like I'm an idiot. "He is an art teacher. There *is* a difference. He had to give up a few things, you know."

"I'd rather drive a tour bus."

Ring has to stop and think a minute before he goes on. "So it was almost winter when we got to Green Hills, and it was cold. But it was close to the bus headquarters. Josie said, 'This is it. I'm stopping here.' And she went nuts when she saw the old brick schoolhouse. 'We belong here. It's been waiting for us. It'll be like living on an island. I can hang clothes on the line in my slip.' And she went a little crazy, too, when she started fixing it over to suit herself." Ring rolls his eyes. "And Purcell said, 'Best place to live is in a schoolhouse if you've got a kid.' Of course, there was space to paint, too."

Ring laughs out loud. "Seeing all the windows painted on the walls kind of got to you, didn't it?"

"At first I thought your whole family was screwed up."

"Purcell's a good guy. He wanted us to feel at home. Josie was crazy about the idea. She said we can look out but no one can look in. And Purcell said for us to decide what we wanted to see out our windows. Cool, huh? We each picked our own neighborhood."

I guess anyone can paint windows on their walls and see only what they want to see. Ring made it sound so reasonable. But there are a few things he still doesn't talk about.

Ring gives me a shove. "Take that silly look off your face."

"It isn't silly. I am thinking. It's the way you shift things around to suit yourself, like the painted windows. Like you can be Fox and Ring at the same time."

"What's your problem?"

"Why did you call yourself Fox when they found you?" And before he can answer me I say, "And how about last Christmas?" My mouth feels dry and I lick my lips. "Why did you run away? What was the big jolt? You made such a big deal out of it."

Ring is suddenly serious. "It was a big deal!"

"So, maybe there was no uncle, or a dog as big as a horse?"

He tugs at his chin, acting very self-conscious. He looks away from me. He jumps up and starts looking through his binoculars, pointing at the sky in every direction. He yells, "No."

I wait for about five minutes. I sit there like some kind of dummy, and then I decide to go home. But when I start to get up he says, "I don't want to think about Christmas. Christmas is a bummer. It's a mean time for me."

I yell at him, "Ring!"

He comes back and stands in front of me. He speaks slowly. "A crazy Christmas card came in the mail, addressed to Fox. And the postmark said, 'North Pole.' A lot of little kids get mail from the North Pole, only I'm not a little kid. There was a message, too: 'See you soon.'"

"So what's the big deal!"

"It shouldn't have come! There's nobody named Fox!"

That just blew me away. "You talked about him all the time. You told a million stories about him."

"Yes, I did. But Fox just kind of came to me when I was a little kid. He was a real person to me. I figured I wasn't alone when I had Fox. I kind of hung on to him when I got older. I don't know where he came from, somewhere in my head, I guess. I could talk to him when I needed someone."

I try to keep a poker face so Ring can't read my feelings.

His voice gets real low. "Maybe, when I was lonely."

"Who would send a Christmas card to Fox?" I speak in a whisper.

"That's the trouble. Who knows? But that part doesn't matter now. Maybe one of the kids from the boys' zoo or someone who heard my Fox stories. People do connect things."

Ring's face is all squeezed up. He doesn't open his eyes again until he starts talking. "It was right there under my nose all the time, how freaked out they were about me and what I had done to them. You can't guess the lies Josie had to tell to get me into school. But they just went kind of bonkers when they saw that Christmas card. It was like the bogeyman jumping out at them, reminding them we were probably wanted in ten states and someone had found us."

Ring took a deep breath and let it out easy. "It didn't take them long to get over it. They didn't want me upset. Purcell figured it was just someone's idea of a joke. They tried to act like it wasn't a problem, and Josie said, 'Your stories about Fox must have backfired.'

"Anyway, I can see they feel bad for making such a big deal about it, and Purcell said, 'Let's forget about this for now. Some day we'll get it taken care of.'

"Only I couldn't forget. I had this lousy feeling about what I'd done. And I know it was right there under their skin all the time. It wasn't working. I didn't belong there. I was hurting them. And that's when I first started thinking it would be safer for them, and less trouble, if I went back to where I came from.

"And then crazy things kept happening, like that guy at the carnival by the dunk tank. I didn't think I knew him, but he kept staring at me and talking and I couldn't hear what he was saying.

He scared me, and I was beginning to get edgy about everything."

"I know you were awfully interested in the pictures of kids on milk cartons."

"You didn't have any idea, did you?"

"It was odd, is all I knew. Did you ever get to Chicago last Christmas?"

"Yeah, we did go. Purcell had to pick up a bus, and he said the three of us would go in and celebrate Christmas there." And before I could ask, he adds, "No, Ben. No dog as big as a horse. But it was a fun time. The best. We stayed in a motel near the airport. The planes just about took the roof off every time they flew over. We'd go to movies in the afternoons, and every night after we'd eaten supper we'd take a walk along Lake Michigan. The wind was wild, but it didn't matter how cold it was if Purcell wanted to walk. He lived on a lake once in Wisconsin. It didn't matter if the waves were washing up against the wall spraying you. The last afternoon before we went home it was cold enough to freeze your face, and Purcell wanted me to walk with him. Josie didn't want to go.

"I felt like I had icicles down my neck. When Purcell saw me shivering, he pulled up my collar, and he wrapped my scarf over my face. He leaned closer to me to keep the wind off. Once he put his face close to mine, and he said, 'Don't you worry, you're never going to leave us.' We walked along quietly, then he stopped. 'You're my son. We won't let anyone take you.' And he pulled his scarf off and wrapped it over my shoulders, and he held on tight to me. Ben, I about burst when he told me that."

I don't have anything to say, and I don't look at Ring. Instead, I look over at the bushes where he hid the Baby Ruth candy wrapper.

Ring nudges me. He is smiling, but I know he is through explaining.

We start for home, and when we crawl over the fence out of the swamp, the sun is going down, a circle of fire, and the sky is flaming. Ring looks through his binoculars back over at the swamp and at the sky, then he swings around to look at a flock of swallows diving, little specks in the sky. And then he brings his binoculars down and looks at me close-up until I push him away. But he grabs me in a bear hug, and I can hardly breathe.

Chapter 26

But there are some things that Ring doesn't talk about. Like the little flyaway bird in his room, the bird that was in his pocket the day they found him.

And then one afternoon, just accidentally, I overhear him talking to Mattie. It is a couple of days after our trip to the swamp. I've been busy all morning running errands for Kate, trying to find someone to paint the upper part of our house. I guess she's expecting me to paint the lower half.

When I come in the house I hear talking in the kitchen. The voice is so low and private sounding that at first I don't know it's Ring. I go to the door, then I stop.

It is Ring with Mattie. "You know, when I was

a little kid I thought it was a real bird. Like it got hatched from a regular egg. Isn't that crazy?"

I back into the shadow of the door. Mattie is tilting her head up to look at Ring. I'm almost afraid to breathe. I don't want them to see me. I probably shouldn't be listening, but I can't help it.

I watch Ring take the bird out of his pocket. "You know, I really don't know for sure where I found this old bird. See, there was a Christmas tree in a department store. I hid under it, I remember. I was really little."

Mattie pats Ring on the knee.

"But I didn't see any others. This bird was alone on Christmas, as far as I know."

Mattie whimpers like a little kid.

"So I probably stole it off the tree."

Mattie gasps as if she is going to swallow her tongue.

"That's the only place it could have come from. There was a lot of Christmas music, over and over, loud. I wanted to hide from it. It scared me."

I hear Mattie clucking like an old hen.

"I must have been there under the tree staring at all the flashing lights until I went to sleep. The next morning they found me. They said I had candy canes in my pockets."

Mattie claps her hands, very pleased.

Ring holds up the bird, and Mattie and I are both looking at it. "It's a tree ornament. See, it's special, Mattie. I think it was company for me that night so I wouldn't get scared."

Mattie reaches over and touches the bird as carefully as if it were alive.

"Anyway, they let me keep it. When I was older I thought maybe someone gave it to me, someone special, someone I didn't remember. So I was real hyper at first, kind of superstitious about the bird. I made up all kinds of stories to suit myself. When no one came to get me, I always wondered why. For a long time I was sure somebody must be looking for me. They must be somewhere." He leans his head close to Mattie. "Maybe the bird knows."

"Maybe the bird knows," Mattie repeats.

When Ring straightens up on his chair, he's taller than Mattie standing in front of him. "It's too late. I don't care anymore. I honestly don't care."

Mattie runs to the pantry. I can hear her banging cupboard doors, and she comes out with a fistful of cookies. She holds them up to Ring. "Eat!"

"See, I was always looking for someone. I don't now." It's quiet for a few seconds. I can hear Ring chewing away on a cookie. "Now I just want things settled for Josie and Purcell and me."

Mattie goes after another handful of cookies.

"I was just about this big, Mattie." Ring points to his knees. "This tall. Dumped in the toy department at Peterson's. It was my pride got hurt, Mattie."

Mattie holds his hand. Then she hugs him so tight, her skinny arms stick out like chicken wings. Ring has to stop talking for a minute. I am ashamed now for listening.

In a minute I hear Ring again. "I had my picture in the paper. My social worker showed me my file one day to prove that everything had been done to find my folks. There was a newspaper clipping with a picture of a little little boy. And underneath: 'Who is this child?' It said no signs of neglect or abuse, that I was very bright. That the only word I could say was 'Fox.' No one ever reported me missing. But someone must have known that I called myself Fox." Ring pauses a minute. "Then I was put in foster care."

I start backing away from the door. I see Ring hold out the bird, and Mattie takes it in her hand

and lays it against her cheek. The bell makes a squeaky half chirp. It makes her laugh, and I hear Ring laughing with her.

"It's a present for you, Mattie."

I sneak out so no one will ever know I heard.

Chapter 27

School is closing in on us. Ring hangs around with me and helps me paint the trim on the house. We don't talk about serious things like his personal life anymore, not since that day at the swamp. But my big question remains unanswered: Does he still belong to the state of Ohio or to us?

Purcell has given up driving a tour bus, and he is back painting and teaching. Ring and I ask him to paint a picture of us with the whooping cranes. Purcell says he first needs to see the whooping cranes for himself. We can't wait to bring him there.

Anyway, things have slowed down, simmering

without much happening, a kind of stillness like the wind dying down after a big storm. When Meeker stops by to see Kate and me, he says the quiet spell is good for all of us. Kate's glad Meeker still comes by. So am I.

But Ring is still acting like nothing is for sure, kind of antsy. Some days I don't think he'd recognize a fly on a picnic table. So I try to be extra cheerful.

And then all heck breaks loose all of a sudden and everything spills out. Josie and Purcell come over late one afternoon. It is hotter than a baked potato. Ring and I are sitting on the porch steps trying to keep cool. They come up the walk fast, and they are both looking at Ring. They push me over and sit down beside him. They each take one of his hands, and they are sending him a message. It's in their faces. I see a shiver go down Ring's back.

But nothing's going to happen until Kate gets home from work. Mattie keeps bringing out chairs to the porch until she has ten and I have to help her take some of them back inside. Meeker brings Kate home in his truck, and when she looks around at everyone on the porch she pulls him along. Her hair is soaking wet from the heat, and sawdust is sticking to her arms. We wait while Mattie brings out the fan and plunks it down in the middle of the porch without plugging it in.

Then Purcell stands up and turns around and faces us. His face is pink and sweaty, and a powerful smile is forming. He stands there a minute looking at Ring. "It's done. Our boy is here to stay." He pressed Ring's shoulder, and then he grabs Josie.

And then everyone starts hugging. Kate even hugs Meeker, and Meeker hugs her back. Then they all start talking at once, like starting in the middle of a paragraph, like everyone knows a lot more about what's going on than I do.

Purcell goes right on talking louder than anyone else. "It's a good thing we all went back to Ohio together. It didn't cause so much trouble for Ring or for us." He stops to take a sip of the lemonade that Mattie has handed him. "We ended up in their juvenile court. But, you see, I was there with him. I had written to them, too, about him disappearing."

Ring interrupts him, "And they didn't have to ask me. I told them everything. I tried to explain why I ran away, both times. It was hard to

explain." He ducks his head. He's really embarrassed. His face is red.

And it is hard to explain if you don't know
Ring. First he ran away to catch up with Josie and
Purcell, then he ran away from them—and for
the same reason each time. The way I figure it, he
must love them a lot.

Josie shakes her head. "We had been making
plans with Social Services for Ring. But then suddenly Purcell's work ended, and we had to move
and everything changed so fast. One of the problems was moving a child from one state to
another before an adoption is final. There are so
many people who have control—an attorney, a
judge, and people from Social Services. All I can
think of is how wrong it is for the poor kid."

The door keeps banging as Mattie goes in and
out of the house, stepping over our feet and leaning over our backs to bring us more lemonade.

"I mean, he couldn't come with us." Josie
looks down in the mouth for a minute. Then suddenly she leans over laughing. "I guess he did
come, though, right along behind us." She reaches
over and takes Ring's hand.

They are all talking again about Purcell and
Josie being investigated by people from the Social

Services Department, visiting two times, asking all sort of questions, and looking over the old brick schoolhouse.

"They talked to me," Kate says. "And Meeker."

"They asked me a million questions, too," Ring says, looking over at Josie. "They even talked to my teacher. I wonder what they asked."

I can't help thinking that no one in Social Services bothered to ask me any questions. And I probably knew the most about Ring.

Mattie goes over and sits down close to Ring, and he puts his arm around her.

If they had asked me, I'd have told them some of his wild stories are probably true, at least half true. And I'd want them to know how nice he treated Mattie when she was sad about the dingo dog in the park that got lost and the swans she missed seeing, and about how helpful he was when Mattie got lost herself. And they should know about Ring's big family that includes all of us. That Ring could be my brother. He makes me feel a lot bigger than I am.

And I bet they'd never guess that Ring can fly a plane better than Charles Lindbergh and he never has to leave the ground. And I'd want them to know he taught me how to fly, too, because he showed me most anything is possible, that it is good to dream.

I am really glad that the old brick schoolhouse with the windows painted on the walls and the doorbell on a rope didn't upset the people from Social Services.

So it took all summer, and a lot of fancy footwork, Purcell says. Something that no one wanted to talk about until the waiting was over and Ring could come home to stay.

Now I've got it straight in my mind about Ring. I know why he went into the river and kept going until he disappeared. He was looking for something that belonged to him, a place of his own. And the good news is, he found it.